Judy Millar

THE RULES OF P·A·R·T·I·A·L EXISTENCE

Red Deer College Press

Copyright © 1992 Judy Millar

All rights reserved. No part of this book may be reproduced by any means, electronic or mechanical, including photography, recording, or any information storage and retrieval system, without permission in writing from the publisher.

THE PUBLISHERS
Red Deer College Press
56 Avenue & 32 Street Box 5005
Red Deer Alberta Canada T4N 5H5

CREDITS
Cover Art and Design by Ron Lightburn
Text Design by Dennis Johnson
Author Photo by Ed Jurewicz
Printed & bound in Canada by Best Gagné Printing Ltée
for Red Deer College Press

ACKNOWLEDGMENTS
"Book of the Dead" has appeared in slightly different form in *Secrets from the Orange Couch*.
Excerpts from *Kathmandu and the Kingdom of Nepal*
Copyright © 1983 by Prakash A. Raj.
Used by permission of the author.
The author extends special thanks to Aritha van Herk and Roberta Rees. Thanks are also extended to Alberta Culture and Multiculturalism for support during the writing of this book. The publishers gratefully acknowledge the financial contribution of the Alberta Foundation for the Arts, Alberta Culture and Multiculturalism and The Canada Council.

CANADIAN CATALOGUING IN PUBLICATION DATA
Millar, Judy, 1957–
The rules of partial existence
ISBN 0-88995-083-0
I. Title
PS8576.I44R8 1992 C813'.54 C91-091844-9
PR9199.3.M56R8 1992

For My Mother & Father

CONTENTS

An Introduction
9

ELEPHANT IN TAXI
13

BOOK OF THE DEAD
17

CIRCLE OF EYES
37

SOUTH
59

KICHIKINNY
81

VISHNU'S DREAM
89

HEAVEN, THE RAIN GOD, THIS WORLD, WOMAN
117

THE GOD WITHIN YOU
175

For now we see through a glass, darkly; but then face to face: now I know in part; but then shall I know even as also I am known.
—*I Corinthians 13:12*

AN INTRODUCTION

"What are your stories about?" No matter how often I am asked or how well prepared my reply, that question throws me. Arjun, the self-doubting teacher in "Book of the Dead," hears in a student's innocent question a challenge to his faith. When someone asks, "What are your stories about?" I, too, hear my deep motivations questioned.

Are these stories *about* Nepal? I don't think so. Nepal is their ground, their universe. Its phenomenon is the root of whatever they achieve. But that is something different.

Of her "African" fiction, Margaret Laurence wrote in *Heart of a Stranger*, "The process of trying to understand people of another culture—their concepts, their customs, their life-view—is a fascinating and complex one, sometimes frustrating, never easy, but in the long run enormously rewarding. One thing I learned, however, was that my experience of other countries probably taught me more about myself and even my own land than it did about anything else. Living away from home gives a new perspective on home." Some things don't change.

Some do. Since Laurence's time marginal voices in our community have swelled, demanding hearing. They have reminded us that, while silence is not always golden, the appropriation of an "Other's" voice by an artist of limited experience can be unfair to the very others the artist attempts to hear. Writers especially have been reminded of the responsibility of public voice. Today honest writers must be sensitive to this public feeling. We face the question of how much we allow that awareness to determine what we write and ultimately how we imagine.

Laurence declared of her African stories that she was never absolutely sure she "got it right." I know exactly what she meant. You can research and check as long as you like, and you're never absolutely sure you've got the language, tone, situation, feeling right. But I am no longer tormented about whether I should or shouldn't, can or can't. I quickly saw, in any case, the impossibility of ever fully conveying the life of a country in fiction. I grew, as all writers must, to be satisfied with parts. I have learned that, whatever one *sets out* to write, one ultimately writes one's self. And thus have I forgiven myself for reflecting the very *difficulty of engagement* with a foreign culture, be it strange individual or nation, another gender or generation or an uncharted region of the self.

Tiny Nepal, a sort of "crossroads of Asia," lies on the map like a kidney bean sandwiched between India and China. It is a country less than one-quarter the size of Alberta, Canada, with a population of about eighteen million people. Within its borders Hinduism and Buddhism meet, each undergirded by ancient local animistic and shamanistic cultures. Over twenty ethnic and language groups occupy three main geographical regions, which can be thought of as three bands stretching lengthwise across the country. In the northernmost Himalayan region live the BhoTiya tribes who speak languages of the Tibeto-Burman family. Culturally and historically they are linked most closely to Tibet. The southernmost band, an extension of the Gangetic Plain of India, is populated by Indo-European peoples who practice Hinduism. Between, in the midhills region, live a variety of groups whose languages are of both Tibeto-Burman and Indo-European families. Their religious practices mix Hinduism with Buddhist and shamanistic influences.

On a clear day, flying into Kathmandu, one can theoretically see the entire north-south span of the country, from the highest mountains on earth in the north to the hot Gangetic Plain and rhinoceros, cobra and tiger-inhabited jungles of the Terai in the south. The impassable Himalaya and the malaria-ridden lowland have acted historically as Nepal's border defense, saving the tiny land from the foreign invasion and colonization it would have likely otherwise endured. The country was only opened to Western influence in the early 1950s, when the unbroken power of a century-old succession of hereditary prime ministers was returned to King Tribhuvan, a direct descendant of the original monarch who had unified the kingdom in 1768. Since 1951 various attempts have been made to set up a democratic state, all unsuccessful until only a year ago (after these stories were written), when external pressure and popular unrest finally forced King Birendra Bir Bikram Shah Dev to relinquish ultimate authority. For a country in many ways medieval, it remains to be seen how the party system will work out. How do kingdoms fare upon loss of kings?

What Nepal is to Nepalese and what Nepal is to foreigners are, of course, two different things. Generations of Westerners have grown up with the notions of romance and mystique that books and movies about the East have fostered. God-kings, living goddesses, horizons and paradise lost strike a chord deep within us; they are what we travel to find. When we go we find ourselves not only in another place but in another time. We get more than we bargained for, a world, in fact, we hadn't yet admitted to ourselves existed. I mean that world inland, inside, that outward travel causes us to recognize. When we think we have seen enough and head home, we find home is no longer where or what we believed.

For the writer this process is magnified as she sets out again and again for that strange country, trying to comprehend. Laurence knew this: "And yet, for a writer of fiction, part of the heart remains that of a stranger. . . . The whole process of fiction is a mysterious one, and a writer, however experienced, remains in some ways a perpetual amateur, or perhaps a perpetual traveler, an explorer of those inner territories, those strange lands of the heart and spirit."

Of tourists in his land, Dawa Tenzing Sherpa said, "Many people come looking, looking . . . some people come, see." There are many ways of looking, many things to see. One may, as some do, see poverty, squalor, suffering. One may see romance, smiling faces, charm, magic, physical and spiritual beauty. All of it is there and not there, depending on the extent of the illusion and the depth of the perception. If a cheerful "innocent" face hides extreme suffering, how can I not be moved by the faith, hope and love so deceptively manifested?

As travelers and expatriates, we have to admit that what we are often doing in the East is writing, or re-writing, ourselves through experience of the "other." Western voyagers, resident aliens, what we read in our inner books, as often as not, is our own inability to receive in our hearts the "heart of the stranger." As a writer, I think that very incapacity may be finally the point.

ELEPHANT IN TAXI

In the dream a small terra cotta elephant grows and grows, filling the front seat, then the whole car. Gradually the hard exterior splits; clay sags; fat, muscle erupt under new skin. The skin glows a translucent pink. The great ear flaps back. The eye turns to look. In its aperture God is dancing. Dancing with four arms, two legs. A man comes begging on stump legs, calloused hands. His tin cup rattles the smelly street. Joyful through and over him, God's blue limbs jerk, no, kick the tin cup out of reach. *Dance with me, dance with me!* Then the huge beast and small battered car ignite, motor out of your dream.

This dream is not a picture but a window. The elephant in taxi shrinks, its giant shadow looms. Down, down flies the elephant in taxi, through autumn light, late afternoon. Tail pipe sputting brown lumpy steam. Up, up flies steam, brown smoke, black rain clouds raining black rain.

Along the Ring Road thunders the elephant in taxi. Ever in the elephant's sight, God dances creation. Out of the elephant's eye, like fire—the Valley of Kathmandu. Seven peaks. King's Road. Swayambhu's golden temple. Storming around the open road—God, elephant and taxi. Green paddy, spun field, mud house, bicycle wheel, flung bird jet-still, buffalo, face, tree cart tempo walla. Something blankets the afternoon, a particular smoothness. Black lake of black rain, rising, rising, spills out through the passes, hushes the mountains forever.

Causing you to sink. You stump the mud bottom, your legs black and monstrous. Like bread dough rising, they bulge and thicken. With the garden scythe, you cut off at one hip. Then the other to match. Life juices, pulp, resins—a globe of golden elixir drifts out of reach. What is left: this black sea of pain, which knocks soothingly against you like a cup, smelling of tin.

Who can cleave darkness from light? Who divide a mountain? In comes Manjushri, great God of Wisdom. Heaves his sword over Chobar. *AWKKKK? ZZSSSHHH!* Black slides down the round mountainsides like silk. The valley drains.

Causing you to swim. Up, up, panicked through generations. Your nose stretches and gropes. What does it see? A small terra cotta figurine. Which grows and grows, filling the front seat, then the whole car. Gradually the hard exterior splits; clay sags; fat, muscle erupt under new skin. This lake is not a window but a mirror. Up through its eight-peaked frame you shimmer.

Bihanna. Morning. Assurance of nothing. Cock crow. Dog bark. A smell of cumin. A pink glow. Out on the Ring Road, a pain finding a taxi. You raise all your hands. But your hands are gone. Your eye turns to look. Bits of terra cotta shell, dust glitter, spray from new translucent skin.

Your frozen limbs trickle. Something remembered. Bones and ragged bits fuse and swell. Nerve ends sing to their partners. You grow knees. You grow pads.

ELEPHANT IN TAXI

God dances across the asphalt like a flame on water. A pink car, upside down, screeches around you. Pulls up beside. Four doors, hatchback, gas flap, sun roof, hood drop open on their hinges. This taxi is not a taxi but an eight-petaled lotus flower. So. Eight delicate pink tips. You are hungry.

The elephant has swallowed the dream. The taxi's become dinner. One two three four. Round the tips of the mountains you saunter. North east south west. Your eyes: open wings. Round and around you go, dancing.

In the distance shines a temple. You lift your trunk and bellow your wisdom. The mountains repeat. The temple winks.

BOOK OF THE DEAD

Many years ago in Toronto, CHUM-FM Radio ran a contest. Whoever could, in sixty seconds or less, open the station's safe would win its contents: two thousand dollars. Some Dick or Harold or John cracked the safe and with his prize bought a motorcycle. Years later, the bike long since passed to another owner or trashed for parts, someone asked this John or Vern how it felt in the moment the safe door opened. It felt, said Vern or Ken or Sid, like I was burning up.

Gap

All his life Colin Douglas has waited for this. Waited to rest astride his motorbike, legs planting an inverted V. To look west. The sun, a red India rubber ball, rolls up the B.C. coast toward him, drops into the ocean, igniting the world. Colin waits. The moon, a white disc, wheels down the black sky. Still Colin waits. Just at dawn, for an instant, the sky, the ocean, the ground his feet rest on become one space. The Christian scholar kick starts out of the early morning darkness. Having all his life waited, not pushed, believing life should be lived to the full. And now he is rushing, rushing through the interior toward the thing he is most curious about. Black leather, tall valley encased. In the east, an eerie new dimness. High skies, heavenly peaks. Yet Colin is calm, quietly reverent. Racing toward the thing he awaits. A suspension or possibility, a gap.

Given a window seat by a beautiful heartless woman at the check-in, Kenji Nishimura, Buddhist scholar and quiet wit, contemplates the Void. Eyes the absence between him and the China Sea. Feels himself separating, like an egg lifted high, higher, tapped lightly, the thin clear spinning down, away from the sure yolk at its center. The egg metaphor Nishi dreamed up years ago when he caught himself holding rigid, too distant (at a party? meeting? lecture?) from those he was closest to. Saw himself balancing, liquid, watchful, an enormous eye inside a smooth exterior. Deceptive. Two oceans separate Nishi from earth: one of water, one of light. The sky is cloudless, bright. The plane's engines throb. Nothing. Nothing moves.

Years later, telling the story for the umpteenth time, Professor Grigor Ivanovna makes an unusual leap. Not in the story—that hasn't changed much—but in his memory, normally faultless. Grigor's lips move in the old well-practiced patterns, but his mind is elsewhere, searching for a moment. Those years ago, when he and his brother Yuri nearly bit it, as the Americans would say. Grigor relates the story word for word: how monsoon clouds forced the pilot to follow river courses and roads. Sight rules only in a land without radar. The terrifying buck of the last serviceable Twin Otter in the Kingdom of Nepal. And then . . . that is when Grigor's story takes over, tells itself. But the climax, the core, he somehow can no longer catch hold of. As he talks, progresses smoothly through the details, working himself out of the social spotlight in the same way aid programs claimed to work themselves out of a job, Grigor comes up against . . . what? A space, a gap in . . . memory? Or experience? Grigor can, in fact, *remember*, but the terror, the importance, has vanished. It is as though so many tellings have freed those minutes from his body, dispersed them into thin air.

Seated beside his wife, Carol, on the Delhi-Kathmandu flight, John Hallinan can't breathe. He feels every other passenger staring at him in smug condescension, self-satisfied pity. His chest, his throat, so tight air has to be sucked. Why now? He had suspected, of course, but why tell him now, here? The diplomat cannot decide which upsets him more, Carol's infidelity or her informing him of it here, where he can only splutter with hurt and rage, no door to slam out of, no place to hide his eyes. All he can do is turn away, stare out the window into the boredom of cloud this junk heap of a plane, it seems, will never rise above.

This must be close to hell, thinks Arjun Patak, fingers frozen to the handlebars, thighs sizzling as he pedals up the long hill into Kathmandu. Late fall and already mornings in the valley are shrouded, damp-smelling and smoky. Arjun swerves to avoid a sudden shape that looms not an arm's length from his front tire out of the mist. A faceless woman, her shawl drawn over her head for warmth. That is what people are these mornings—gray insubstantial specters on the fringes of vision. It is humiliating for a southern Brahmin to be seen riding a bicycle. Soon, he tells himself, soon. It won't be long until he has enough saved for a motorbike. Arjun has already persuaded the man not to sell the one he wants, though persuasion was more expensive than he'd planned. Arjun's clients, the *bideshi* house where he teaches private lessons in Nepali, couldn't live much farther from his own. To reach there by eight-thirty, he must get up at six. Bath first, then weight practice until seven-thirty, an hour by bicycle to the far north side of Kathmandu, stopping on the way down Patan hill for coffee in the restaurant of his Indian cousin, Ramesh.

This morning, though, Arjun senses a shift. Inside him something is knocked sideways, displaced, like a bicycle in a high wind. This morning the low-hanging cloud of fog and woodsmoke seeps behind his eyes, obscures knowledge as well as sight: the *bideshi's* house, the house of Frank and Hilde and Catherine and Horace and the rest, has been swallowed perhaps, or never existed, his own destination become less palpable than ever.

Against the wind, in the teeth of God, flapping maroon. Descending the Nangpa-la from Tibet into Nepal, his original home, the reincarnate lama, Tulshig Dawa Rimpoche, pictures himself as a passerby would see him. At first, from a distance, Rimpoche would seem an illusion, a kind of glimmer or movement in the traveler's eyes. Then as he drew closer on the horizon, a shiver of wings, a great dark condor, soaring against the sky. Closer, the single celestial bird would splinter into three. Three walking out of one flying. Closer still, an old gold-habited monk would totter into focus, supported on either side by young monks in wine robes.

Rimpoche sees himself and his escorts, the jagged pearl peaks above them, the blood-colored rhododendrons on the slopes below, all the better for being blind. Overcome years ago by an abundance of light and beauty, he has given up sight easily, as one, upon dispelling the illusion of permanence, gives up groping in muddy ignorance and, freed, swims up into a great ocean of light. Rimpoche senses the passing of souls far below this trail, climbing up from Kathmandu. Sweating porters (his own Sherpa people as well as midhill and lowland natives), trekkers from all over the world—terrified, looking, depending unwisely on their eyes, yak trains hauling the burden of foreign expeditions eager to attain the eternal home of gods by physical ascent.

His escorts steer Rimpoche slowly, safely down the path toward Thame, where he will act as the principal officiant of the annual Mani Rimdu festival. Rimpoche knows this Mani Rimdu may be his last, and the thought fills him at once with regret and profound joy.

OCEAN OF LIGHT

Highway pilot, downhill motorcycle pacifist, Colin Douglas glances back. Highway Number One, Roger's green, green Pass, Mount Bonney, the Sir Donald and Hermit Ranges. More than once Colin has been written about, his maintenance of scholarly dignity and the bike-touring hobby considered paradoxical and newsworthy. He feels suspended now, feels possibility between his teeth, along the fine hairs in his nose. Where the long Connaught Tunnel empties boxcars into blue air, the bike levels out. Ahead, a final downward pitch to the valley bottom.

Another quick look back before he loses sight of them. And now the vision comes. Mount Bonney, Mount McDonald are there *in front*. But behind, oh, behind! Gargantuan. Soaring. Three times as high, like the earth's dream of giants or a family of monstrous ghosts.

Colin's head swivels back to the road just before impact. A car passing below the crest. At fault, head-on with Colin, handsome, blond, forty-two, in perfect health, scholar and loving family man. But Colin does not die. He is still contemplating the vision as the paramedic gives him mouth-to-mouth.

Colin's head is battered, but his body is perfect inside the protective leathers. He is noticing the light in his eyes, a white even light such as one sees at dawn, before sunrise. This light spreads through him like a river, and he is well near home in the helicopter, when the flow begins to pinken, deepen, become red, like the most beautiful sunset he can imagine.

Landed safely in Kathmandu, Nishi watches through his porthole as the All Clear loses effect. Curious dogs, a line of long-skirted women carrying trees on their backs, thin sinewed men in belled trousers and hats like truncated cones stroll across the tarmac. For some, Nishi sees, the runway is an interruption in daily pathways, for others a source of entertainment or livelihood. Nishi feels the dampness under his arms, the air close with the rustle of passengers anxious for release. And now the pilot shuts off the air conditioning. Huge letters sprawl across the low brick building that is the terminal. In English they say WELCOME TO NEPAL. Behind, like a postcard or a joke, soar the youngest, highest, most foolishly beautiful mountains on earth. Nishi catches his suit jacket and his hand luggage as they burst from the overhead compartment and, with a twinge in his stomach, follows the perspiring line of passengers to the door. Bidding an English goodbye to the hostess, Nishi is thrown, rejected fish, into a cool sweep of light, which is blinding, which is noon, which is possibly, then distinctly, breathable.

The story is like this. Grigor and his brother, Yuri Ivanovna, the unstoppable geologist team, were returning from field work, charting stratigraphy in Nepal's midwestern region. It was early monsoon, and they were glad to get out. For two weeks already they had trekked across muddy fields in melting heat to the single grass airstrip within a hundred kilometers and the little wooden shack, where a man with a crackly radio would tell them the plane was coming soon, soon, it was coming tomorrow, it wasn't coming at all. The plane didn't come, of course, not until that day, and lucky they were there, or they'd have missed it—another storm was breaking nearby, and the pilot wasn't going to wait. They were indeed lucky, the pilot said in English (he had been trained in British Columbia he told them). Last year this strip was under six feet of water, you had to walk three days to the next one.

They weren't aloft for long when the clouds began to boil up around them. Without radar the pilot had to fly by what they called sight rules. In the midhills and lowlands, they weren't too worried about running against a mountain, but the sky was wicked, and they were bounced around in the little plane like so much thrashed wheat. They followed the Rapti, Babai and Mari Khola, and Kali Gandaki Rivers for a long time, and then, when the pilot could get a glimpse of it to the north, the east-west road from Pokhara to Kathmandu.

Forever, it seems, they sneak along the edges of storms, picking their way between huge heaped clouds, booming shoals. Finally they turn north, the last stretch into Kathmandu, but the winds are high, hitting them now from the side, where before they rode a tail wind. "Here at home it would've been a snowstorm, a blizzard," says Grigor. The wind whipping the windows like that, you felt you were being pelted, sprayed with . . . what? Pieces of mountains or cloud or the worst-looking demons these people could concoct, spitting at us through their teeth.

Grigor laughs now at this next part, tells how, through the bounced-open cockpit door, he watched the copilot pull back the throttle, the pilot's hand reach over, push it up again. Several times this happened, the throttle being moved one way, then the other. "That's when I knew we were in trouble," Grigor always says, always laughs.

Then his shoulders begin to shake up and down so violently Carol brings herself to touch him.
   –Are you all right?

But John Hallinan is laughing, laughing hard, utterly silent, tears coursing down his cheeks, chin, flying onto his lapels and the dirty napkin still crumpled in his lap from the snack earlier. The plane is stuck, stuck forever in this infernal dirty whiteness. Of course, of course, how could one expect—
–John.
Softly. His name soft on strange lips, tongue. Tongue. Touched, oh, touched, rolled in a strange mouth. Wash your fruit *well*, his mother used to say. It may have touched a stranger's mouth. He shrugs Carol's hand away as though it were a bothersome fly.
Back and forth between Delhi and Kathmandu for six years now, though it seems longer. What were they doing? Playing games everyone knew were games but which were nonetheless vital, or so his government believed, to keep the balance. Courting Delhi, courting Peking, repelling them again in turn, blustering against the Russians, cooperating behind the scenes. Sometimes he wished they would all just meet in Kathmandu and fight it out to the last man. Blow it all to hell and be done with diplomacy, the slower death.
Think anything, anything but this pain. John's mind falls back in the old pattern: too late to turn tail and flee home to the States. There's a point beyond which you never completely. . . . They call this a hardship posting, but the real hardship is return. . . .
–John. Please look at me. At least look.
That is when his eyes go blank, white, and then, it has never happened before, he sees red, literally a wash of blood over his eyes. He is enraged, enraged, and must grip the arm of his seat so as not to lift his hand.

He must look ridiculous, one arm waving in the air like this. If it weren't for their damned dog, thinks Arjun, he would look more dignified entering, like a teacher, not an animal tamer. Arjun drops another cookie in the vile leaping mouth. They say the dog is friendly, they talk to it, clucking as though it were a baby, but Arjun is not so stupid. If this hound is so friendly, why does it leap and yap so, showing its teeth and trying to knock him over? In any case Arjun will not allow a dog to soften his resolve. After thinking it over now for several weeks, Arjun has made up his mind. Today he will ask for a raise and for some security besides. How can he plan for a motorcycle, for example, and pay rent here as well as send money back home regularly to his wife and *ghar* in the south? He must have some kind of written contract, not this wishy-washy so-called gentleman's agreement. Also Sabita, his girlfriend, keeps asking to be taken to this movie or that restaurant, and in addition he would like to buy some good jogging shoes. Life in Kathmandu is not getting any cheaper.

Yes, today, in the conversational part of the lesson, he will turn the subject around to money and the need to earn a decent living. With this firmly in mind, and after the niceties of tea are over and the usual thickheaded number drill has been repeated again and again with no progress apparently in his students, Arjun broaches the subject of their morning activities, asking them questions, teaching new vocabulary along the way. Then they are to ask him. And he tells them. "First," he says, "I bathed myself, then I weights (as in English) lifted and jogging ("jogging") went. *Tara,* but my running shoes no good are and now my leg sore is. *Dukha,* yes, *dukha,* sore."

Up to this point, Arjun is quite pleased with himself, the way he's directed conversation so smoothly. But now something goes very wrong. One of them, Horace, asks in English why Arjun bathes first, *then* jogs. He should do it the other way around. For once Arjun does not know what to say. Lately he himself has been thinking the ritual morning bath has lost its meaning, but this is not something he planned discussing with Horace or any of them. Arjun pulls back, giggles a little, embarrassed. In the silence that follows, his students begin to shuffle and look at their watches. Arjun declares today's class over, having lost the will to pursue the issue of the raise. There is always tomorrow. Arjun bids them all a cheerful goodbye and remounts his bicycle, bound for the office where Sabita works.

As he pedals Arjun can't get this business of the bath out of his mind. In fact this very thing was bothering him so much one day he had gone to call on a friend who knew something about Christianity. Perhaps there was something in it, something he missed following the same old way of life everyone followed here. This friend told him he had just been reading about something called the leap of faith, which, he said, the author described as a kind of jump across a chasm you couldn't see to the bottom of. You started from the place, he said, beyond which you couldn't actually point to anything tangible, but then, on the strength of this faith, you leaped out into thin air. That was what these Christians did apparently, dove into space with no clear idea of where they would land. Did they think something would catch them? Arjun wondered. "I haven't got that far," replied his friend. "I'll let you know when I find out."

The mystery play tells of the coming of Buddhism into Tibet over fourteen hundred years ago, when King Song-tsen Gam-po built Tibet's first Buddhist temples, flooding light upon a land of barbarity and spiritual darkness. The play is allegorical, also telling of an individual's awakening from illusion.

As Rimpoche enters the courtyard to be seated on the elevated dais, a novice monk sounds the conch, which, like the incarnate lama, forever returns in a widening helix upon itself. As the conch sound curls again and again around the listeners, Rimpoche generously resumes his body after its previous death, returning to teach the world and his disciples.

The conch music fits pleasingly in Rimpoche's ear. One day he will return to study from this conch blower. For the teacher has much to learn from the former student. One bright day Rimpoche himself will blow the lowly conch, light the sacrificial butter lamps as the esteemed lama arrives. Then the world will be drenched in light.

The full-cheeked conch blower, the flickering butter lamps, the dais he is seated on, the maroon-robed monks, the excited local people crowded along the walls and balconies—Rimpoche sees without need of eyes. Like the other devotees, Rimpoche waits eagerly for the dancers to appear.

One Flying

An eclipse, then in Colin's eyes, gratuitous, like the black rush of snowsheds in June. The greater exhilaration is in entering, for at that moment the bike is lost, as are the hands, the feet, any part that is grounded, touching. Everything lifted, rising in flight. Only the mind clings to memory, the rules of the road, the safe exit returning ahead. In the snowshed, but for slatted dimness, nothing exists.

The mind clings even when breath is cut off, muses Nishi. This dream I brought from Japan still alive, still possible . . . and mocked by choking heat. In the alleged inefficiency of this country, in a battered Datsun with a hired local driver, Nishi is already leaving the Kathmandu Valley behind. They are driving south, almost to the Indian border, toward Lumbini, the birthplace of Buddha. If it was hot landing at midday in the Valley at forty-five hundred feet, it is hotter descending to the low plains of the Terai. Nishi's pants and shirt sag against his skin. Sweat and dust vie with Buddha for his attention. When the body slackens, the dream carries on. Nishi watches the green scenery and the greasy back of the driver's head with equanimity. He speaks silently to the head:

I can't breathe for heat, yet you propel me forward still.

Then unexpectedly the head turns, following something for Nishi's benefit. It is a young woman swinging between rows across a field. Or is it the building behind her, which sports an English sign, LUMBINI GUEST HOUSE? Nishi nods politely and smiles. The driver smiles back widely, more widely it seems than the U-turn skid the Datsun performs, dust from the back tires becoming a distraction across their faces.

But expression inevitably changes, and Grigor's audience becomes quiet, as he himself does, so as not to miss the next part. Finally they are about to land. The pilot turns north—there is only one runway—as far into the wind as possible. Not far enough. They bump and squirm closer to the ground, the back wheels quiver above the tarmac.

This is the moment Grigor cannot locate. The moment he made himself think about the physical action of a strong crosswind on a small twin-engine aircraft. If the front wheel touched down first? What lateral force would be exerted on the aircraft's tail? How to stabilize the wings? Then, like the hands of pilot and copilot, stability is irrelevant, for the small aircraft leans over, way over, on one wing. Through his window, sky, clouds above him, above them all, where a moment ago houses and trees bounced. A distracting noise now from the opposite wing. On his side Grigor feels nothing, lifted high and veering, a miraculous soaring bird without benefit of logic or sensation. But he registers a cry from the direction of the scraping wing. His brother lost somewhere on that side, the wrong side now, of this plane. Later these seconds looked to Grigor black and terrible. Now, telling the story, he no longer inhabits them at all.

The black wave recedes. In that fluorescent cabin, John remains conscious, unconsoled.

–I love you.
A pattern in the upholstery. Over borders this fingernail shall not slip. Fine tickle. That corner. Missed it, did we? Again.
–Did you hear me?
Lobsters. Not lobsters, crabs. But huge . . . they could have been lobsters. Bought a dozen of them from a fisherman on the long spit road. Ate all twelve between the two of us. Ate till we were nearly sick, washed down with wine, then made love. That night a hurricane up from the Gulf damn near blew us away. Tent flying straight up over the dune and out to sea, outstretched stranger chasing white wings.
–For Christ's sake.
–Don't say that, like that. Just don't.

The catch is in the leap. Arjun looks down at his knees pumping. What if a hole opened up in the road ahead of him? Would he dare? Would he close his eyes, pray to . . . whom, Jesus Christ? Oh, yes, the catch is there for those aware of it. The catch is one's question, one's doubt. It flashes upon Arjun what a terrible dilemma these Westerners with all their practical knowledge are in. It is why they are always walking around with a scowl perhaps. They are thinking about what lies ahead, straining their eyes to see what is inside the gloomy hole yet hoping to outdistance it, too.

A clash of cymbals heralds the first dancer. *Clang! Clang!* The dancer whirls around an altar containing the symbolic objects of sensory perception: a mirror representing sight; dough cakes, taste; burning juniper, smell; silks, touch; and a book representing the mind. His own cymbals betoken sound, which the dancer offers up sacrificially, as all other sensory instruments must be sacrificed to free the individual from material association, the first step in awakening.

Rimpoche follows the action closely, the long golden robes serene as his facial expression. From the deity house, a group of lamas emerges next, come to transform the indigenous beliefs of the people. Buddhism came to Tibet as enlightenment comes to the person, not by destroying but by uplifting. Rimpoche nods imperceptibly at the dancer's fine headdresses, whose crown of fire represents the light of illumination, not material combustion. Three skulls representing greed, anger and ignorance are consumed in this light. When these emotions no longer control action, vision becomes true.

LUNG TA (WIND HORSE)

When he looks back, the tunnel becomes a prison. Something pushes one through—ah, helpless. Colin Douglas lies motionless in the Foothills' Intensive Care. They landed on a white cross painted on the pavement. Elevated his stillness through all living things. Blood, oxygen, the electricity of the body, *Miami Vice,* afterbirth, reflection, crutches, a child's face, *Time* magazine, midget, *Friendly Giant* rerun, chrysanthemums Dierdre lunch newborn Godzilla saltines Women Macintosh PC indoor-outdoor Scheme-a-Dreamballoons Archie dilation episiotemy contraction heartbeat giggle pianoscream hometown hands monster leg stump Demerol furnace hell bruise burn bone fingernail, earlobe, baby tooth, skin, skin, skin, knee, navel, womb, wind.

Still Colin does not die.

Was the revolution deliberate? Swung around the opposite way, they are no longer in motion. Instead they are stick figures rasped by dust. Nishimura cannot tell whether this has been a joke or a near accident. He catches sight of *lung ta,* Tibetan prayer flags, torpid in the steel lowland heat. The driver restarts the engine, and they drive back the way they came, then veer onto a mud track. Ahead a prayer flag collapses on the faded *lung ta* printed there; the horse does not fly but limps.

In a shop next to the monastery, under a belligerent sky, Nishi bargains unsuccessfully for a wheel-of-life *thanka* (he will try again back in Kathmandu) and purchases a fixed-price copy of the Tibetan *Book of the Dead,* with which he is already familiar (he left his copy at home in Tokyo). He has an urge to read it now, with its practical and compassionate advice to the deceased to be read as the body burns on the funeral pyre, warning of the ever more terrifying visions it will encounter on its journey toward rebirth. Nishi finds comforting the admonitions to remain undisturbed by these visions and the deliberate enlightening passages meant to focus the reincarnate's mind on the ever-present possibility of liberation from illusion and impermanence.

Back in the raging car, Nishi tries to imagine how it would feel to vanish, to go from being something to being nothing. First the white cell from his father would descend from his crown *cakra.* Then the red cell of his mother would ascend from his navel. When these met in the heart *cakra,* a white even light would spread across his eyes, turn gradually to deep red, then total darkness. At that stage, if Nishi were advanced in tantric practice, he could bend formless, colorless, empty space, the most subtle state of consciousness, to meditation on *Sunyata,* absolute emptiness. Nishi closes his eyes against the scenic whir outside the taxi. . . . No, it is impossible. Lurching inside the speeding Datsun, he feels more like a slightly overweight, unmistakably fleshly consciousness entering the most difficult phase of rebirth. In the *bardo* or gap body, one is propelled helpless on his karma toward a new and possibly unpleasant future.

The time may have come to stop telling this story. He cannot sustain the terrible flying moment because he is finally bored. Bored with the whole incident. Grigor puts his empty glass on his host's coffee table, dons his coat and descends several flights of stairs into the Moscow night. Their gasps, sympathetic noises bulging, as always, in his ears. It is sad about his brother, yes, but that was never the point. Tonight, out of the story of loss, Grigor has at last plucked the kernel of his dissatisfaction. He feels lighter, as though he has released an unwanted burden far above, among the glowing guests.

Though relieved, Grigor is not relaxed. His long legs scissor the darkness, driven by a physical urge or some other force. It comes suddenly then, just as Grigor steps impatiently across a curb. Helplessness, pure terror. Northern pavements unresolved as Asian winds. The face behind the windshield white, hilariously frightened. A witness would later testify the deceased had appeared drunk.

There is nothing left now but prayer. She will leave him in the end, and the children will forever look at John askance, project a kaleidoscope of folly on his face. Jesus Christ. The words he took for granted as a young novitiate, before Carol, before anyone. He and the other boys in the refectory making jokes of pious Latin: *Noli me tangere.* Don't touch me. The time he and Dick MacNulty wore shorts and running shoes under their cassocks and after matins stuffed the cassocks in a hole in the stone wall, sneaked over the top and ran a marathon before the word was popular, twenty-six miles as near as they could guess, to the next town, their heels kicking up freely behind. They were tired, exhausted, but laughed and laughed at the end, salt of sweat and tears running into cracked lips, hands dropping naturally to their knees, bellies heaving in and out. Jesus Christ. Out there, Woodstock, Vietnam, and they escaped the monastery riding the curl of New Jersey forest, riding the white line over secondary road that at the time seemed a freeway.

So John prays, silently, quickly. He remembers the old prayers, some of them, but they will not do now. He was always a reformer, favored Vatican II. His prayer now in the vernacular of his present life. *Please God, don't let her leave.* Then, after a moment, *But do what is best.*

He takes the shortcut from Naxal to Kanti Path, passing through alleyways that open onto bumpy mud tracks over lush paddy fields, a complete rural landscape hidden from the street. Out on Kanti Path, Arjun finds himself caught in slow traffic. Normally he would push and weave through vehicles, animals and people, but today it is impossible, or else he has lost the desire. A jeep honks loudly, roars behind him, then pulls out to pass. In that moment, appeasing an instinct long buried, Arjun grabs its fender. Swept up, torn back and forth among honking taxis, tempos, bicycles, rickshaws, cows and pedestrians, Arjun ponders faith anew. This leaping business, both act and concept, may be beyond him, though truly Arjun seldom has found anything beyond his ability or understanding. Then what of the One and the multifaceted familiar gods and goddesses, like family, who have known him so long? Arjun lets go of the jeep and bumps to a stop in the cobbled entrance of the motorbike shop. He hadn't planned this interruption in his journey to Sabita. But a quick look now, knowing the money is coming along, is sure to make him feel better.

But the soul's balance sometimes tips too far. Thus a skit to discourage overpiety. In the skit a very stupid Chinese monk confuses his devoted student-straightman with erroneous instructions. In his clenched fist, the monk dangles a rosary before the terror-stricken student. "*This* is how to count prayers," screams the monk, blasting the beads, *zik zik*, along the string. The student-everyman, attempting to imitate his teacher, fumbles with the beads, then drops the rosary on the floor. The monk raises his stick and beats him. *Whack! Whack!* "Idiot! I see counting prayers is beyond you. Then show me how prostrations are performed! That is surely simple, even for such a fool as you!" One eye on the monk's stick, Everyman scrambles to his knees. Shaking violently he proceeds to collapse flat on the floor, hands over his ears. "Fool! Fool! Fool!" screams his teacher and drives the groveling man off stage. Everyone explodes with laughter, including Rimpoche, whose robes billow and wheeze.

FALLOUT

Inside the tent, Colin is resolved. For days now, heart swelling to a beat not its own, lungs pummeled into performance, Colin has lain without motion or conclusion. Now Colin waits merely to be ready. At 5 A.M. he feels ready. Seconds later his wife, Marion, bursts into the room, having dreamed on her hot cot down the hall of an explosion.

At first Nishi thought the taxi had blown up with him inside it. But he quickly saw this wasn't so. Then where is his driver? And unless he's mad, there *was* a hell of a bang. When they pulled up to his hotel, the Annapurna, the driver jumped out quickly, helped ferry Nishi's bags up to the entrance. Nishi had come back for the last one and was reaching across the back seat to get it, one knee caught painfully on a broken spring, the other foot lightly toeing the ground behind him—when the air changed.

Where was his driver? He wanted to pay him and check into his hotel, get settled in his room after this long, long day. He was pulling back out of the car, wrestling his suitcase across the seat, when it all sank in at once. The screaming, the shouting behind him and a familiar word in English heard some moments ago that he only now took in. *Bomb.* Nishi let go of the bag and turned quickly, just in time to note something familiar on the landscape—his driver's head.

Now he lies face down in his new room at the Yak and Yeti on the hastily arranged bed. When his driver and the others blew up, he hadn't known what to do. His own upraised arms had cradled Nishi's head. He had done what he could, but really what could anyone say or do?

The ghost of Grigor Ivanovna hovers somewhere in the Valley, supremely grateful to have landed on the safe side of death. Despite outraged editorials in *The Rising Nepal* decrying thugs, revolutionaries, murderers and disturbers of the peaceable kingdom, a smug certainty hangs in the air, along with Grigor, waiting to be discovered.

As usual, the first and last to know. Here news travels tongue-quickly but to those without the tongue. John Hallinan's chin sweats on the mouthpiece of the office phone. He is holding for his British counterpart on the other end, busier, it sounds, than he. The wet stickiness makes his chin itchy. Voices fade in and out on the line—excited and frantic, squealers and peacemakers. One or two he thinks he may know. Outside, the embassy garden bobs in a light breeze, then grows still. John frowns at the clarity of yellows, reds and greens caught frustratingly in moments past, dead as photographs. The voices become one mouth with many tongues. Well no one can say John Hallinan doesn't have his ear to the ground. For it seems to John this whole beautiful, sorrowful, wickedly beguiling little nation is whispering in his head.

Arjun doesn't know what to think. Not one but three separate explosions, people are saying—at Singa Durbar, the palace gate and the most serious at the Hotel Annapurna, where among others the obsequious doorman was blown straight up through the roof. Arjun had heard rumors that something like this might happen, but so had everyone for some time. It was no secret, the increasing unrest of the socialist Congress party, the communists and other suppressed anti-government elements. You could read about it in the palace-controlled daily newspaper, between the lines. The king himself had been ordering arrests all over the country as a kind of preventive measure. None of Arjun's friends is among the exploded people, not even any friends of friends. Of course he worries about the future, who doesn't? But when you come to it, there's not much a person can do.

Up in his mountains, both inside and outside the realm, the reincarnate Rimpoche spends extra time in meditation. Violence he knows may provoke or defuse. But as a means to an end, it is always wrong. He asks his monks, when a flight comes in, to bring him news. Someday if he or his successor keeps at it, a road will link this remote valley to Kathmandu. It's always best to change with the times even if it means a paradise somewhat soured by smelly fumes. It is simple: you change or die. Mani Rimdu over, Rimpoche readies himself for the journey home. Already he looks forward to next year.

Some complained it was an inside job, that no one could crack a safe that quickly unless he knew the combination. But Sid or Dick, discovered twenty years later in a roller skating palace by a roving reporter, denied the accusation. He still remembered the combination though. Would the reporter like to hear it?

CIRCLE OF EYES

Despite her name, Kumari is not a virgin. A tidbit, irrelevant gossip. But it sticks to Clarence as a bit of litter might cling to one's shoe. Perhaps it is as his colleagues (or more accurately their wives) claim: Kumari is more than "help"; she is like a daughter to him. Clarence stands with his back to the mirror looping his tie. In recent months, since the rapid deterioration of his eyes, he finds it easier to lean against the bureau and dress by feel. Now the most difficult part: fitting the long end through its own loop without losing the shape of the knot or, worse, dropping the whole thing. Bad enough that he's had to give up the much smarter Windsor knot he used to wear and go to this sloppy style. But now this has become a challenge. . . . Well he was never like some who could knot a tie blind; he'd always used his eyes. Clarence finds the loop with his little finger and shoves the tie end through on the third try. He feels around his stomach for the two ends, gauging their relative length, then pulls the short end through the loose knot, working the knot up to the neck button between his collar ends. He remembers to breathe. Clarence expels a long lungful of air, ready for the day. On his way out of the bedroom, reaching for the sports jacket he shaped around the chairback yesterday, Clarence exhales loudly again. Of course, how stupid of him to forget. Dr. Joshi called yesterday to cancel today's meeting. Joshi was required to be at the airport today to welcome the returning King. Clarence feels at his throat for the carefully made knot, pushes the offending fabric against itself, unwinds, flings the tie impatiently across the jacketed chair. There's no use getting angry, he knows that. It used to be these inconveniences slid easily from him. Lately, though, he feels them adding up like weights around his neck.

Is it the project that tires him? Has he been knocking himself out in Kathmandu too long, trying against the odds to help? Perhaps a time comes when one has done as much as one can. . . . If the condition were not congenital, his eye problem might even be a kind of sign. But Clarence has known since he was young that, like his father and his father's father, he would someday go blind. Macular dystrophy was rare both in frequency and effect. Starting from the middle of one's sight, the blankness gradually spread outward so that the last thing to go was peripheral vision. His case as yet not too advanced, Clarence can still orient himself in the space around him. But his view of the world has changed. Now people and objects extrude from the dark perimeter; colors, shapes burst from the world's sides.

It is absurd, then, the decision he makes now to spend the lost day in a bookstore down in the close-walled heart of Kathmandu. For he can no longer see to read. Still there is so much more to books than just the words inside them. Clarence loves their smell, its dignity and sadness. And the feel of paper under his fingers. Even before his eyes caught up with him, he would feign blindness, try to guess from the feel of the paper a book's contents—thick rough-edged pages could mean early Himalayan adventure, while onionskin whispered poetry. Clarence enjoys poetry; he is particularly fond of Wordsworth. One poem especially stays with him, its sentiment anyway, if not the actual lines: that while youth climbs mountains, age is wise enough to contemplate them from below. Clarence feels he would like this for an epitaph, that he has moved from the first estate to the second honestly and with grace.

So Clarence embarks on his favorite journey—up the uneven muddy laneway from the house, then a left turn on to Kanti Path, which will take him down into the tight pulsing district of Asan Tole. He fingers the flashlight in his pocket, wonders if poor eyesight and poor lighting in the shop will at last deprive him of this special pleasure. Still, released in the sun's warmth, Clarence daydreams of the three-tiered shop. From the street the place is small and unremarkable. Inside, though, wind endless cobwebbed passages of musty books— he doubts whether over the years he's found them all.

But here is Kumari again, unbidden, winking in the back of his mind. *Lined up outside her door.* That is the phrase he heard yesterday, accidentally, from the office of a junior colleague; the young wife and a friend were conversing inside. Household gossip seldom reaches Clarence's ears; what does is generally dismissed. With his eyes getting worse and the new necessity to remember, not read, Clarence has no time or space in his crammed head for servant intrigue. But these rumors of Kumari will not be ignored. Which *door* did they mean? Anywhere near the house, suitors, or worse, would be obvious, if not to him (since strangers wandered freely in and out of the compound to visit the servants) at least to the servants themselves. Do they *line up* while he is consulting at the university hospital or department of health? Clarence quickly rules out this possibility; his comings and goings are unpredictable even to him. No, it is all silly malicious gossip. The fact of Kumari, well into her twenties, as yet unmarried and with no apparent intention of doing so, would make these simple folk suspicious, require bold stories to explain. Pleased with this sensible explanation of his own, Clarence speeds his steps. Though he cannot see them, he can hear the occasional flapping of bats in the huge plane trees outside the royal palace, hundreds of bats dangling like black fruit from the branches above him, waiting for dark.

Quickly Clarence crosses Kanti Path, trusting rickshaws, bicycles and taxis to avoid him—so far they always have. Reaching the opposite sidewalk, he begins to walk west along the sidestreet that leads to his bookshop. It is four short blocks to the shop, which will be on his right, just past a shoemaker. He'll know he's getting close by the *ping ping* of hammer against sole. On the third block, a small boy taps his leg, chants, "One rupee!" Clarence finds the boy's dark head in his stifled eye, ruffles the hair and smiles. The urchin's mouth dissolves into a grin. The mischief of an old man's touch.

But here, four blocks counted off, Clarence has reached neither shoemaker nor bookshop. He walks a block further, hoping he's miscounted, knowing he has not. Has he turned too early, too late? Is he north or south of where he should be? Clarence walks on, steps more carefully. His large head sways from side to side, centering a marginal world.

Moons grow and darken under Clarence's arms. If only Kumari were here with him, he thinks, the yellow morning splitting under hot white noon. Beautiful Kumari with her dry jokes and her unusual voice, her English. Clarence turns Nepali phrases awkwardly over in his mind; he could ask his way in English, and somebody would answer. But his feet carry on through progressively narrower passageways and their intersections—a dissemblance of periodic brightenings, irregular assertions.

A woman, fresh cow dung dripping from her fingers, scurries through a corner of Clarence's eyes. The brief sighting fills him with hope. The woman seems a good omen; there is something eternally comforting about the sound of cow-dung patties slap-slapped against a wall to dry. After this it does not surprise him to emerge into the largest open space he has encountered since the main road. He stops, grateful for the relit sun and for something else, a deeper resonance in the day. The Great Bell tolling in Hanuman Dhoka. He has come too far south, then, past his destination. Continuing, Clarence resolves to turn left, east, at his first opportunity.

The heat, the long dusty walk have made his legs tremble. If he can just find a space, sit a minute. Instead he feels new density around him, sees movement—limbs, colors, faces — disconnected, like a dream or the disturbing rock video Kumari brought home when he first imported the VCR. Kumari. Clarence reels back a step as if knocked, then recovers. Wakeful exhaustion. Where is she, where? Dawn filling his window with twisted branches. Then the soft turn of her key in the front door. Gillian! His little girl. Not little anymore she kept reminding him. Eighteen she was then. Her mother snoring softly beside him in bed. What struck him most was that Gillian got up with the rest of them for breakfast. Chatty, apparently unfatigued, she slid a fried egg on his toast in that careless but dextrous language of wrist and spatula. How many years . . . and he can still picture the egg, its yolk perfect if a little pale, the white crisping into brown at the edges. Just an egg—vulnerable somehow, exposed, but mocking, too, with that yellow eye.

Clarence aches all the more for recalling how he ached that long-ago morning, not for the loss of Gillian, he sees now, but of Gillian's mother. Peggy left him the next week while he was away in Geneva organizing a delegation of health officials wanting to visit Mother Theresa. Everything had fallen through, the planned tour of Asian hospitals and homes for the dying scuttled by a record-breaking snowstorm in Europe and the unforgiving schedules of the most crucial delegates. Then, at the last minute, Mother Theresa herself proved impossible to track down. India, it seemed, was having its own problems. Flooding in the north had triggered severe outbreaks of cholera and typhoid; the bird-boned saint had flown to that most newly opened mouth.

When Clarence returned defeated to Edinburgh, the unthinkable had been thought. That was the worst, not that Peggy had moved out but that she had thought to leave, planned, probably even as she was driving him to the airport. At the check-in counter, before the professionally patient agent, her calm confident hands had tagged his luggage, printed the tiny name and address, pulled the piece of paper neatly through the loop of elastic, let the world know he was all thumbs. He had always been proud of her composure before he arrived home to that proficient absence.

Something jogs his elbow. His head cocks. A child shouts, and a word, a name, flies up like color. Kumari. Clarence feels dizzy now, soft-boned. His skin pricks up. Kumari. That word.

From the shadows where they prepare her, the girl would often gaze across Basantapur Square to Trailokya Mohan, where oddly costumed foreigners perpetually rearranged their legs. She would ponder these legs—each day different but always long, always doughy and soft. Now, behind closed eyelids, she speculates on the legs. She wonders if there is a connection between the length of the legs and the paleness of the loungers' skin. Lately she believes there is a connection. It has something to do with blood or, more precisely, lack of it. She must sometime ask her tutor if this paleness were not caused by a poverty of blood to color so much skin. The girl giggles to herself, in love with her madness.

"Be still," cluck the women, "be still." Darting squirrels. In their center the twelve-year-old girl, whose name for as long as she can remember has been Kumari and who is a living goddess. A thumb smooths down the nervous curve of her eyelid. Now the eye jumps under the thick grease pencil. Three strokes black its half-moon, the last pressing out beyond the lid's outer corner, through the hollow there, tickling along her temple all the way to the tip of her ear. Nib at the inner corner, caught, teased briefly by flirtatious lashes, stroke stroking the fine lower edge of her eye to its outer rim, completing the circle. A sting, then, before she can blink, the cold Essence of Sublime Beauty Drops, which will cause the pupils to flow over the iris and transform day vision to night.

Thus, with heavy eyes, regal robes, high-piled hair, the golden snake of fortune twisting on her neck, the Kumari waits in the shadows. Watches the square below. A man in a white shawl. The beggar team—one pushing the cart on which the other, legless, rides. Both wear watches. And Adidas, one on his hands. They go by here every day, several times. They make Kumari laugh, make her happy somehow. She slips them rupees anonymously now and then, through the servants, for she is not permitted to leave this house. A group of women, ragged, thin as twigs in garish saris, rustle by. They have come from the south, India perhaps, looking for the young goddess Durga, called Kumari, in whose manifestations this valley is rich. Gradually more people fill her small square of vision. They linger, squat, smoke. A cow ambles through the square, its ribs projected like a blessing. A woman toting a frayed bag of vegetables glances up, and Kumari retreats quickly. She must not be seen—yet. A white man with white hair, his steps alternately cautious and quick. He reminds the Kumari of a goat pulled on a rope to market, unsure whether to shun or embrace the day.

Soon they will be coming to collect her, escort her down the stairs and install her in the receiving throne on the main floor. There she will give tika to the King and receive a gold coin in return. Then they will ride out together through the streets in the golden chariot. Once, on this yearly pilgrimage (for so it seemed), Kumari spied a sign over a restaurant: THE HUNGRY EYE. Watching the crowd gather, her eyes burn with greed—no matter how many people cram her vision, there will never be enough. Kumari would like to move closer to the tiny window, open up this boxed view, let in more light. But she dares not lest she be noticed either by her guardians inside this house or worshippers outside. Her feet are getting sore standing here, her knees collapse a little under the ceremonial gown. Where are her women to take her from here? Kumari feels too warm, hot. She sways slightly on her feet, blown but rooted, like a half-grown tree. The heavy paint presses her eyelids down. Shapes float, insubstantial, across the window, bodies flicker on white light. Where are her women to rescue her from this place?

The beggars again with their Adidas. The aliens with strange pale legs. The thin black women hoping for redemption. The shawled man. Six men who push a cart of meat through the scene discard themselves, leaving a vision of wheels. A coming together of spokes at a hub. The sahib with a sadness burning out of his angel's head, soft cow dung, the woman carrying vegetables who might have seen. How did Kumari come here? She doesn't remember. Sitting between candles on her throne. Yet in her eyes these visions linger.

Now, too, night vision visits her, and the door to the inner passage is revealed. The goddess's pupils dart left, right, eyewhites poking darkness. The Kumari brings a slow jeweled hand to her lap. Lifts it ever so slightly above. Presses her abdomen with red-painted fingertips. There, like this morning, the sweet sweep of pain. But she does not wince. The

Kumari knows the wisdom of the jungle, the value of a pure face. Hushed, behind eyes, she waits.

For two hundred years, they've stood outside her door. Lined up across the centuries waiting to receive tika and her blessing for another year. The elaborate virgin, their parade together through the streets (crowds whispering, *Did you see the goddess? Did you see her eyes?*) seems to the King like the Gurkha regiment in this nuclear age—handsome but obsolete. Educated at Eton College and then Harvard, His Highness is a worldly man, disdainful of such barbaric practices, ignorant superstition. When, about ten years ago, His Majesty began to doubt, he bought the dark glasses he wears now. Specially designed on the cutting edge of technological advancement, the glasses, called Photorays, came from America, where great scientists invented a lens that changes color according to its sensitivity to waves of light. But sometimes, the King has noticed, even the most sophisticated technology could use some work. Right now for instance. He has entered the dark passageway that leads to the Kumari, and his glasses are not yet changing. So he stands in the chilly gloom waiting for the lenses to clear. His foot begins to tap on the floor, ringed fingers drum his thigh. Such nonsense, all this. If he were not already tiringly familiar with this place, he would be forced to feel his way ahead in the dark. As it is, he knows exactly what he'll find: an ancient wooden door, whose deep-carved convolutions swallow one's fingers whole. His hand retreats instinctively to a pocket on the kingly thigh. In any case, someone should put in a light and a mirror; he'll see to that for next year.

It's the blooming dark that creates these hallucinations—in America someone is likely studying that. For as always ancestral faces begin to appear. At one time, before he threw away ignorance and followed the tradition of scientific Truth in the

West, His Highness believed these kings were him, previous incarnations of him and he the foreordained monarch of his time. Now he knows such quaint beliefs are delusions of the illogical mind. He is only surprised how widespread such ignorance can be. The King is aware of such things as causal factors—not magic or sorcery—now that he has a degree. If he is reigning monarch, it is for some other reason than recirculating genes, some fortunate conjunction of the stars. Probably he deserves the honor, has earned this right. The King has not yet worked it out that far. As for these apparitions, they are an optical illusion, the psychological effect of darkness upon the mind. Or perhaps there lurk some bad germs in the air, which, breathed in, cause some weird chemical effects in the brain. Whatever the cause, the ancestors appear.

First his father in full regalia poking thoughtfully at his incisors with a long ivory toothpick, looking sideways in the dark. After him, King Tribhuvan, best loved and remembered for overthrowing the Rana family—a royal revolution. Now he stands slouching a little at the shoulders, tired looking, with deep crescents under his eyes. It is said that the year he was to die, the Kumari was so sleepy she put tika by mistake on the brow of the Crown Prince, whom the King had brought along. Sure enough, they say, within the year the King died, and the Crown Prince stepped up to the throne. As if a little slip of ignorant girl could predict such things. Why, back in those days, she would not even have had the benefit of tutors or education, as the Kumari has today. A long pause, then Pritvi Shah, blown up grandly with conceit, Great Unifier of the Malla kingdoms. And last, unrepentant as he is responsible, a joke fanned by his sweating punkah wallah, Prakasha Malla, the last of that long line of Mallas, whose supposed indiscretion has led to his presence here before this damnable door. For around that last Malla, the uneducated masses have inextricably wound an old wives' tale. While praying to a beautiful goddess, they say, this Prakasha Malla had indecent thoughts. Angered, the goddess appeared to him and announced that from then on the King must worship her in the form of a virgin Buddhist girl, the Kumari. Each year in Indrajatra, he must receive tika from her and thus gain her protection for the following year. In return he should give her a gold coin. The embellishments went on: if the Kumari cut herself as a young girl or lost a tooth and visibly bled or when she started menstruating at puberty, her time as a living goddess was up, and a new Kumari had to be found. No one would marry an ex-Kumari; it was believed that the man who broke her virginity would die within the year.

But these days the world had no place for such snivelers. The laws of civic and international life are no different than those of the jungle; to survive one must trade fear for cunning, one must be bold. His father's tale of hunting the Bengal tiger was a case in point. For many years the Great One had eluded him. But one day, riding to hunt upon his elephant, his father surprised the tiger consorting with his mate in a quiet glade. But the old tiger, wise to hunters, was quick, and his father's shot merely grazed its foreleg, leaving the beast slightly wounded but now in a terrible rage. Instead of fleeing, the beast turned face, lunged at the elephant's hind leg. Again and again the King shot at the tiger, but the elephant, lurching and plunging in fright, pitched the King about so wildly it was a feat merely to hold on to his gun. The bloody mouth snapped and slavered. The King pumped one bullet after another into tree trunks, into grass, into thin air. Finally his elephant went down, snorting and bellowing in her own blood. The King, forced now to dismount, used the elephant's thick body for a shield. Over her screeching, king of men faced king of beasts. The king of men had one bullet left in his gun.

The elephant heaved between them. The tiger crouched, ready to spring. The King steadied the gun. His fingers twitched wildly, but his head had never been clearer. When father told son the story, he would linger on this moment, eager yet reluctant to release it.

The beast draws back. The King's fingers whiten. The cat's body quivers with intention. The King tightens his aim. Now the tiger falls back on his haunches as though bored with the game. But the King is not fooled. The Great One is midflight when his heart explodes.

His father had brought the tiger's skin home, of course, where for many years it was proudly displayed in the main reception hall of the royal palace. When he was a little boy, the King would beg to be told the story again and again. Now, standing ready to worship the Kumari, the King sees more clearly than ever its point: it is useless to be grand like the elephant if one is a coward at heart; success crowns the man who, over the terror-stricken body, keeps steady his sights.

At the window of Kumari Devi, had she seen movement? If so, it meant good luck. If not, well . . . Kumari lowers her eyes, flips long black braids from her shoulders so they fall, red-threaded, down her back. Dangerous trying to glimpse the Kumari's face. Reversing the natural order. For though the virgin-goddess is worshiped to cure bleeding and infectious diseases, it is well known she can cause vomiting, bleeding, even miscarriage if a person looks into her eyes.

But Kumari is bold, bolder than she maybe should be. She knows people talk. Well let them. Perhaps they have reason. She is young, after all, but not too young, and beautiful, as boys' eyes have told her. They imagine she is shameless, arrogant. They imagine she is better off than they, working as she does inside the sahib's house, showered with presents and leftovers. Lately she has noticed men spit in the street after she's passed, averting evil. But who would she marry even if she could choose? These city boys are no less coarse and wearing than the ones back home.

The vegetables tug at her shoulder, and the day is still young. Kumari steps off the curb and shouts down a trishaw. She bargains fiercely with the skinny youth, coaxing him down so smoothly, smoothly, then pushing even lower to a ridiculous price. The boy, fed up with such keti-sahibs, stands up on his pedal to ride off. "Tik! Tik!" she yells after him, for her eye has settled in a fine curve of his cheek. "Panch rup, siddyo," she proclaims, already in the seat. "Tik *chha*," the boy's head jerks. It is more than the original price.

Nearly as fast, Kumari is stopping him again. "Wait here." Stuffing rupees in his hand. She motions to the vegetables on the seat. "Eat some if you like." Then vanishes through a dark expensive-looking doorway, leaving him to wait on the busy street.

She liked the look of the boy; when better to have her fortune read? It is the tourist palm reader she has chosen because she's heard he is the best. She is given a sheet by the assistant at the door. Kumari doesn't read English well but slowly makes out: "Lalji only gives reading in English." So far so good, Dr. Clarence would say. Then the price—fifty rupees an hour. Kumari checks the number with the assistant even though she is good at numbers. Checks her purse. An hour will be plenty.

Fifteen minutes later she is back out on the street. It is not her past Kumari wants to find out about but her future. And she is not sure exactly what "personality" means. She climbs up behind the grinning boy who has helped himself to a tomato. "Where to?" he asks, red juice squirting up his cheek.

As the trishaw bumps her homeward, Kumari digs in the waist of her sari, pulls out the movie video she picked up at

Supermarkit. James Bond, her favorite: *For Your Eyes Only*. Kumari is not so much for the Hindi love movies as she used to be. And Dr. Clarence will sometimes join her for James Bond. He can't see the beautiful girls anymore, though, he says. He means this as a joke, but Kumari thinks it is terribly sad for a man, even one as old as Dr. Clarence, not to see beautiful girls. So she describes them to him: this one with nice rounded hips and brunette, that one with excellent fair skin and hair like gold but too skinny. He chuckles softly when she tells him this, a rare smile that warms the damp flicker of TV.

The trishaw passes the Russian embassy, which according to Dr. Clarence is full of spies. That wouldn't be so bad but for what he calls their "eyes." Looking up you can see them, long bonelike sticks of metal, which seem to turn in circles randomly like the antennae on a fly. In the evening, though, it is fairly certain these antennae will face the direction in which their magic interferes with the TV. But for now Kumari likes their silvery cool pattern against the glaring sky.

The boy touches his head as they pass the little shrine by her gate. Balances on swinging pedals as Kumari climbs down. Since she returned from the dark doorway and climbed up in the seat behind him, his neck has been burning. He pulls out the cigarette a friend gave him this morning. Coughs twice. Another trishaw passes the other way. "Got a light?" the driver asks. The boy gives it to him. Kumari is almost to her gate.

"What is your name, then?"

Kumari lets down the vegetables, turns slowly to face the boy. He leans back against the strut of his canopy, one foot resting on the handlebars. For a second, Kumari looks directly in his eyes, grins, bends over to retrieve the bag—the video digs a little in her stomach—and stands up.

"Miss Mawnipenni," she says because something inside her grinned also and stood up. The boy's foot slips.

Underneath him his legs pump predictably back to his rank by the Hotel Crystal, but his thoughts keep veering away like specks that disappear in the sides of the eyes. The beautiful girl, the rupees, the tomato, her strange voice and even stranger reply. Something about these belonged together, was there inside him, already known. She had winked at him before turning away, then, when he turned away himself, shouted after him again. Somehow he knew she would do that, shout. Knew the particular sounds—as in a dream, incomprehensible yet understood—that would flow around him, who swerved away from prying eyes. *Yew awnly liiv tweyss.* Suddenly the boy is surprised by this thing he is doing. It is, yes, a kind of miracle, how, between each thrust of his leg, the bicycle-rickshaw glides. *Yew awnly liiv tweyss.* And so now, between each of her words, how many might lie!

In the corner of Kumari's eye, the little shrine beckons. "Ah, Ganesh," she says approaching the stone, a little rice in her hand. "I've not forgotten you." Protector, like Kumari, of the Valley itself—how could she forget? He, too, would ride out today with Bhairab—the Kumari's god attendants. The full-eye moon seeing all.

Back in her village on full-moon nights, Kumari loved to walk. To step softly along the path leading up the hill behind the house. To look down on its blind blinking eyes. This was where she best loved to be, unseen by any but the whispering spirits of rocks and trees. High, higher she climbed, deep into the pine forest and the perfume of rhododendron that would fill the head, if you slept, with magical dreams. In the forest she was never afraid. Past wood sprite or snuffing beast Kumari slid easily, safe in reverie. Above, the moon winked along the upraised limbs of trees, shunning embrace. Kumari loved its round open eye. For the moon asked nothing of the earth but cast its pale light freely. Stark shadows thrown down by the hot aggressive sun, the moon gently dispelled.

Here in the cool dimness, Kumari would listen to the forest creatures talk. Their talk was of the moon or intruders, of the lust night brings on. The talk was soft or harsh, sung or whispered or screamed but always true. They spoke directly, avoiding each other's eyes, while down below in the houses, the talk was all of marriage, bride price, lineage, duty and family life, what a person should do. Talk was indirect and hushed when Kumari walked by. Even her best girlfriend hinted and hinted but wouldn't name the groom or the wedding date fixed by Kumari's family. All around the village, all over her body, Kumari could feel the weight of eyes. Eyes. Glaring, blinking. Since she was a tiny girl, Kumari has been terrified of eyes. Then, before her mother and then her father died, she had lived somewhere in this city with them—an only child. She was three or maybe four—no one could remember—when they led her along the cobbled streets to a great square filled with huge pagoda-roofed houses. Other mothers and fathers led their little girls, too. Kumari remembers waiting (for what?) outside one of the big houses. She was watching a gecko that clung to the wall. She noticed vaguely that the gecko looked odd, the color and texture of brick. Then she laughed and clapped her hands—she could see right through! She tugged on her father's hand. But her childishly delighted laughter was already bubbling away, for her father pulled her along inside the dark cold entrance. Then, where she could not see him, he let go of her hand. She was shoved by him or some other man into the darkest place she'd ever been.

Suddenly under her bare feet, something slippery, warm, congealed. She looked down but, of course, could see nothing. Something ran up between her toes. She began to dance in fear, picking her feet up and up, but wherever she stepped she felt the warm sticky substance. She was terrified, so terrified her tongue locked. She danced and danced, and now she was drowning in blackness—she had no sense of walls or ceiling, only the stench and ooze between her toes.

Then a flash—what? It was as if she'd looked at the sun, then closed her eyes. Another, another—eyes, in heads, the cut-off furry heads of beasts. Everywhere. Enormous disembodied heads. She was stepping now on their flashing eyes, their ears. Their blood squooged all around her. Their yellow eyes flickered on and off, and they made terrible sounds. She covered her ears with her hands to keep out the groaning screeching cries. She closed her eyes against their piercing stares but could not keep them closed, for she would slip and fall, and to fall in all that blood and fur was unthinkable, unbearable.

Still she did not make a sound. Somewhere in her flooding chest and throat, her tongue had drowned.

Hours later, it seemed, a stranger grabbed her hand. Before her a door opened, and her eyes jerked closed with the sudden light. Her knees were collapsing beneath her. She didn't know who she was. When her father came up to her, he looked like another man.

Thus had she been chosen the Kumari, for, faced with the terrifying buffalo demons that she herself, as goddess Durga, had slain in another life, her face had not crumpled with fear. She had remained silent, passive and, they thought, unafraid.

When at the age of twelve she began to bleed, she was led out of Kumari Devi toward home in a small procession, laden with gifts and a promissory note setting out terms of a small pension she would receive for life. That year, her mother and father died of a fever. Her mother's sister's husband came into Kathmandu and picked her up. Ever since, she had lived in his small village, which felt like home. Ever since, he and his wife had been trying to marry her off. Yet her name was Kumari. Kumari, Kumari. If not Kumari, then who? All her years spent in the name of the goddess-virgin. And then one day, the sun fierce as usual, no different from the day before, a jealous gossip hints a boy is chosen. . . . Then what of Kumari? Should she change inside her name then leave it somewhere on a rock like a fickle snake slinking out of her faithful skin? It seemed to Kumari her whole life was about to be sprung, and she herself was a trap set and baited long ago in her youth. Not until she spent an entire secret night up on the hill did Kumari see what she must do. Had she not saved a little pension? She smiles softly to herself. And here she is in Kathmandu.

As soon as she got to the city, Kumari could see knowing English was now the ticket to good jobs. There was a school for English, but she had no money for that. So Kumari lingered at the tourist spots offering the pale gangling foreigners guide service or just asking if they would speak to her for five minutes to help her practice her English. Sometimes Kumari would get well into conversation with a tourist, using all the most polite greetings and big words, when the tourist would frown, as though puzzled by the things she said. After the first time or two, Kumari learned to ask, "Speak English?" right away. For some of these tourists were apparently as ignorant as she. They came from places called Doichlandt, Frohns, Italya and Daanmark. Sometimes one of these foreigners would claim to speak English, but she couldn't make out a word. These ones, she found out, most often came from Dyeownundah, a sort of magical island at the bottom of the world. Their tribe was Kangaroo. Even after a year, Kumari couldn't tell who spoke English beforehand; with their rough skin, thick noses, light hair and round eyes, tourists all looked the same to her.

One day she was strolling down in Asan Tole, eyeing some good-looking oranges in a fruit seller's basket, not really looking out for English tourists, when an older white-man tourist approached and asked her in strange Nepali for directions.

"Speak English?" she asked him right away.

"Oh, yes, thank goodness, yes," the old man said.

And Kumari had walked with him to the bookstore he was looking for. She herself often paused outside its door wishing she could read. Any language—but English would be best. Then before she lost him, she struck a deal. She would help him with the local language, which he said he wanted to learn, if he would teach her how to read. When he hesitated, as though uncertain, Kumari said, "I am excellent cook and housekeeper, too." She was amazed, stunned, when he said yes—and turned out to live here in Kathmandu! For though everyone here wanted to go to America or one of those places, Kumari herself was a bit unsure. Even still Kumari sometimes can't believe her luck. Here she is, the house girl of a great white doctor-sahib who is a kind gentleman to boot. No more for her the roving eyes and clicking tongues of boys on the street.

Kumari hoists the bag of vegetables up in front of her and holds it in both arms. She turns her back to the entranceway, ready to thrust her bottom against the obstinate tin gate, when a taxi draws up with Dr. Clarence inside. Again Kumari puts her bags down and hurries to open the car door for Dr. Clarence to get out. "Thank you, thank you, Kumari," he says and pays the grim-faced driver, Kumari notices, more than she makes in a week. "Let me, let me," says Dr. Clarence as Kumari reassumes her groceries and reverse position at the gate. He fumbles the handle down and punches with his shoulder, letting them both through.

It is odd for Dr. Clarence to come in a taxi; usually he likes to walk. But Kumari doesn't say anything about it until Dr. Clarence himself begins to talk. "Oh, Kumari," he says flopping down on the couch inside the house. His face is swollen, pasty looking. And she can tell by his watery eyes he is not seeing well today. His shirt collar is undone one more button than usual, salt has already formed lines around the sweat mark on his back. Dr. Clarence laughs a little, but it is not a belly laugh.

"This morning your Dr. Clarence wished you were with him. He had quite an adventure, your Doctor-sahib."

"Adventure?" Kumari doesn't know the word.

"Hmmmm? Oh, never mind that now, Kumari. Could you get me a cup of tea?"

Something strange has happened, that's for sure. Kumari flies into the kitchen hoping tea will revive Doctor-sahib. When she comes back with a pot of good Ilam, his favorite, and some special cookies she's been saving from his last trip to Britain, Dr. Clarence is asleep. She sets the tea and cookies down on the table, fixes a pillow under his snoring head, which has fallen back as if severed from his neck. The head is heavy to lift, full, as Dr. Clarence once said, of weighty things. Gently Kumari lifts his crossed feet and pushes a footstool underneath. Then the pink-sari'd Kumari ripples into Dr. Clarence's bedroom. She roots in his top drawer until she finds them. Back with her slumbering boss, Kumari carefully inserts the ear plugs in his ears. Now she takes the video from her sari waist, approaches the VCR, plugs the cartridge in the rectangular hole and presses PLAY. She removes her slippers, lifts the already poured cup of tea and sits down cross-legged beside Dr. Clarence on the couch, facing the TV. Some words appear magically on the opening scene. Just then Kumari thinks of the sun on Dr. Clarence's face. She springs up from the couch to the window to close the blind. But instead she stands transfixed. All around the house, around her and Dr. Clarence, winds a bright circle of eyes. Jai, the gardener, his trowel midair, pauses at his roses. Vishnu, the chaukidar, smokes on an upper step, smokes and watches. Raam, the cook, stroking young cornstalks in the garden, squints away the window's reflection. Even the old neighbor, his legs smoothed like wings on the roof parapet, peers down on her miracle.

Unmarried perhaps, but not unacquainted with irony, Kumari giggles. Giggles because, from her game of hide-and-seek downtown, today's fortune may be cast as bad or good. Kumari hooks the little ring with her index finger and pulls the blind down.

SOUTH

(for L. S.)

Stella's thin fingers drum the steering wheel as Lorna climbs in. Lorna can see the blue *M* of veins in Stella's left hand. For a long time, they ride in silence. Finally Lorna says, "The veins on the back of your hand look like an *M*."

To her surprise Stella answers lightly. "*M*. Mmmmmm. Mother."

"Mud," Lorna replies.

"Mmmmilk," returns Stella.

"Mountain."

"Moon."

"Mmmmerican."

"Cheater. Mary."

"Masala."

"Mantra."

"Motor."

"Mother."

"You already said that. Map."

"Mmmm—" Stella laughs. "You win ya little creep. Gawd! It's like playing monkey-in-the-middle." Stella means the driving. On the road in front of them, men and women, children, chickens, goats, dogs and cows endlessly meld and part.

"You mean dodge ball," says Lorna. "Monkey-in-the-middle tries to get the ball."

"Yeah, well, if they don't get off the road, I'm going to get them." But the car purrs gently by some red-ribboned girls waving from the ditch. Stella waves back and grins. "Gawd, don't you just want to steal one?"

The road is narrow, built high up on a gravel bed. Green rice paddies roll out on either side, forming low hills where they bump the horizon. The smooth expanse makes Lorna think of lawns.

"Lawns," says Stella. "Now there's a weird idea." That frightens Lorna a bit. Her head is splitting with sun.

Stella continues. "Speaking of the Shankar . . . "

"Were we?" Lorna is blinded by sun. Sweat glues her ribs to the vinyl seat.

". . . the name's appropriate . . . " Stella says.

The Shankar has a big lawn, perhaps the biggest of Kathmandu's hotels. Lorna is still trying to make the connection.

" . . . considering how I spent the weekend."

"At the Shankar?"

"Fucking like dogs, Friday till Sunday. Monday, ah, we were completely wasted. Ravenous! Pigged out all day. The next morning, Tuesday I guess, I rode with him to the airport in a taxi and threw up all the way back. Food poisoning. Imagine this: Indian taxi driver, right? 'Most fortunate husband I am thinking.'

'He's not my husband. Aaaagh. . . .'" Stella leans out the car window and clutches her throat to demonstrate. The car swerves. Lorna grabs her seat. Stella pops back in.

"'Unmarried lady, isn't it? Very pretty.'

'No.'

'Yes. Very pretty lady.'

'I'm not unmarried.'" Stella leans again, puffs out her cheeks and presses a finger against her lips. "Then he asks me what my husband does. 'He's a brain surgeon,' I said."

"You told him that? A brain surgeon?"

Stella breathes loudly out her nose, a kind of half laugh, half sneer. "Hnnnnnnn . . . yeah, specializing in transplants." Stella whisks a hand over her head and makes a sound like jet propulsion through her lips.

"So who was this dude?" Stella's vocabulary is metal on Lorna's lips.

"Hnnnnnnn . . . Bruce. Can you believe it? An Aussie." Stella listed people in her address book by nationality in case she forgot their names.

"Blonde?"

"Yeah."

"Hrrrmmm?" Lorna gestures with her hands.

"Yeah."

"Chauvinist?"

"Balloonist. He was here looking into—"

"Don't tell me. Balloon rides to Everest." Stella does not respond. "What about getting pregnant?"

"Hnnnnnnn . . . you mean as a diversion?"

"No, I mean, don't you worry—"

"No," says Stella and swerves to miss a chicken.

According to the map, they are following the Bagmati River, though Lorna can't actually see it. Ahead, the blue curve of mountains narrows, drawing the Kathmandu Valley southward like a funnel. Beside her Stella is all limbs, performing an intricate dance with steering wheel, gearshift and guidebook, thumbing over pages and occasionally, when someone steps too close, standing on brake and clutch. Now she mashes the guidebook flat against the wheel with one hand and fumbles in her purse with the other. Just as Lorna reaches to steady the purse, Stella retrieves a set of blue glass bangles. They look awfully thin and delicate.

"The custom—the rumor is they wear these things from one end of conjugal bliss to the other." Stella thumbs the bangles over her outstretched fingers. They make a high tinkling sound. "You should see how they put them on." Stella yanks the wheel over. The car bumps to a halt just short of a reclining cow.

"Give me your hand." Stella wraps her own around Lorna's. She squeezes the base of Lorna's thumb and little finger together until her fingers meet at the center line of Lorna's palm.

"Ow!"

"Hnnnnnnn . . . that's how you have to get them on. Even then they have to push and wiggle. The idea is to get the smallest—"

"I *get* it, Stella." Lorna glances at the cow—just inches from the fender—casually flinging dirt along her spine. "May I remind you of the penalty for cow slaughter?"

But the engine already races under Stella's foot—and now she's fighting with a sticky gear. The blue Toyota lurches, lolls back in its own churned-up cloud. The next thing Lorna knows, they are ascending. Her feet itch with dust. She does not need to look to know that behind them the distance is filling with snow.

Lorna wanted to drive north toward the sun-drenched Himalayas, somewhere high, where they could get a view. "What's the use looking if you can't touch?" said Stella. She had a place for them to go instead. Mountains, too, but to the south, accessible by road.

Now that they are closer, Lorna can see the range, round and wooded, rising in dark folds from its own shadow on the landscape. Fields crowd uncertainly around its base, pile up on one another in terraces. It seems to be getting warmer as they drive, though she reasons this is unlikely.

"'It is said that people who happen to be holding a cow's tail at the moment of death have precedence in the place of divine justice,'" Stella reads to Lorna from her guidebook. (When Lorna once mentioned Stella's awkward toting of innumerable guidebooks, Stella said she was an "insatiable student of life.")

"Does that mean they come first, as in 'first served,' or they actually get a better deal?" Lorna asks.

"Beats me." Stella flips the page. "Nope. It doesn't say anything about people who die of bacterial infections."

It is not absolutely certain that this is what Lorna has. Not much showed up in the lab. Lorna herself finds it increasingly difficult to tell sickness from heat. She thought the drive might do her good, but now she is not so sure.

Everything is darker now that they're in the mountains' shadow. Around them the slopes grow steep and bare and finally erupt in vertical rock walls on either side. Over the blue hood of the Toyota, the road heaves and twists. Finally Stella pulls over in the only spot available, a small bulge in the asphalt where the cliffs relent. "We're here."

"Where's here?"

"Chobar Gorge. It's supposed to be beautiful."

Lorna is relieved. It will be good to get free of the stuffy car and stand on solid ground. She throws open her door. Black water rushes between her legs.

"Look out!"

Lorna hurls herself back into the seat. "My God, Stella. What in hell are you doing?"

"Hnnnnnnn . . . I didn't think you were going to leap out. I parked near the edge so we could get a better look."

Gingerly Lorna looks down. It is a stunning sight. A ray of

sun slices between them and the canyon wall opposite, throwing a bright coin on the river below.

Stella rummages in her purse and pulls out another guidebook. "It's a 'Lonely Planet,'" she says then begins to read aloud: "'Chobar Gorge. According to legend, when the valley was a lake and Swayambhu an island, Manjushree, the God of Wisdom, struck the rock at Chobar with his sword and released the valley's water. With the water thousands of snakes are supposed to have been swept out of the valley—leaving behind the snake king Karkotak, who still lives close to the gorge. . . .'" A cool breeze gusts through their open windows. "Shall we go on?"

Daxinkali temple is at the bottom of the hill, set back in a grove behind the gorge. Lorna follows Stella down some steps to a small stream. A man stands up to his knees in the water. His dhoti is covered in blood. In one hand he holds a kukhri and in the other a freshly killed chicken. Blood, caught in a slow eddy, pools around his legs. He does not appear to notice the two women.

Lorna turns back toward the stairs. Stella can watch the butchery if she likes. Lorna climbs, afraid to look back. She hears Stella's thongs flip behind her, then stop. Lorna turns. Stella is bent over in a clump of sal, throwing up.

Later they sit beneath a large pipal tree on a stone bench overlooking the stream. The man with the chicken is gone, but Lorna thinks she can see a brownish swirl where he stood. Stella thumbs a third guidebook Lorna hasn't seen before. Then, finding the page she wants, slumps into herself with a satisfied sigh, to read.

"Listen to this," Stella says after a moment. "'Dachsin Kali or Daxinkali, translated literally, means South Black. It is, in fact, the designation of a temple located near Pharping, south of Kathmandu, dedicated to the terrible goddess Kali, destructive aspect of Durga, the all-powerful all-loving mother goddess of Hindu belief. Goddess Kali hungers constantly for flesh and blood, and is easily angered by neglect. Worshippers therefore must assuage the hunger and thirst of this ravenous goddess by regular offerings, usually goats, chickens and other domestic animals. It is said that in the past, human beings were also sacrificed occasionally, but this practice is outlawed today.'"

Stella stops reading aloud, but her dark-pupilled eyes begin to ricochet in their sockets as she reads on. "Oh, Gawd," she says. "It gets worse."

"What?" says Lorna. "Tell me." But Stella does not speak again. Instead she hands the book to Lorna so she can read for herself:

"'Some of the old people here will tell about the days in their youth, when human sacrifice was still legal at Daxinkali. Some say that at a certain temple in the valley, human sacrifice is still performed according to ancient Tantric rites. Children, especially young girls, are warned not to wander alone, for a girl may be hypnotized or spellbound by the magic of certain holy men who will spirit her away to a secret place in the jungle, where she will be trained in Tantric rites and prepared for the day when they will lead her to the temple for sacrifice. After she is sacrificed, the yogis, by a secret process, reduce her body to powder, which they burn for sacred incense.'"

"Perfect."

Lorna's skin slides. A man is standing behind her, almost over her. She has to lean back to keep her nose out of his thigh. He does not move away, though, and she is forced to squint skyward to see his face. But she can't see it, not really—he keeps swaying off the sun.

"Mmmm," she says, noncommittal. But her thighs are shaking, her buttocks tingle, cold. *Perfect?* What does he mean?

The stranger pulls an elaborately carved pipe out of the pocket of his jeans. A thick jet forelock falls over one eye. He brings a booted foot up between her and Stella on the bench, digs in a small leather pouch at his hip. The boot flexes beside her, catches the edge of her skirt, but she says nothing. She is watching a small movement of his throat as his tongue probes the stem of the pipe. He sucks hard, holds his breath for a moment, then lets go. A foul wind rushes up Lorna's nose. A violation, but a man can't help foul breath. *Perfect.* Lorna considers the word. *Per–fect.* A virgin's body ground into incense. Was he reading over her shoulder? *Perfect.*

The man is not native to this country but is local, Lorna thinks. The way he fingers his pipe, leans over his perched leg—he looks comfortable here. A person can't help his looks, menacing though they may be. Billions of people, after all, have black hair. Black eyes, blotched skin, thin lips—none of these means anything. Lorna lifts her chin. Fear is unreasonable. The stranger knows the culture here. He has something of interest to say.

"Kali's underrated," he says and grins, "by people who should know better." The black eyes fasten on her. He pronounces "Kali" not with a short *a*, as she would, but with an *uh* sound: *Kullee.*

"Oh?" Lorna is polite.

"Tourists, visitors like you," the stranger says, "come here to see the goddess drink her fill of blood, then go home clucking like the chickens whose misfortunate partition they've just witnessed." The man leans forward, and now he hisses in her ear. "It turns you on, you see." He grins that awful grin. "But Kali does not leave. She is always here. Kali, the double demon goddess"—a loud clap, Lorna jumps—"never dies!" His hands have come together behind her head. "Do you know what she really likes?" Lorna is silent. Inside her chest her heart begins to rise. "Black male animals, uncastrated." The stranger lets his foot slide, stoops over and lumbers along behind the bench like some great slouched beast. "Especially the humble water buffalo." He begins to sing a weird snaking tune: "'Mountains of flesh and seas of blood, mountains of flesh and seas of blood.' You know what that is?" Lorna shakes her head not knowing what else to do. "It's the song the executioners sing in the streets during Dasain, Kali's festival. Then hundreds of buffalo gloriously die." The man draws a slow finger across Lorna's throat. "Their throats are slit." He puts a hand on the crown of Lorna's head and pushes back. "The head is pulled back as far as it can go. The higher the blood spurts, the more meritorious the sacrifice. Meritorious," he repeats, "you know what that means?" He lets go. Lorna's hair seems to crawl down her scalp. "And after the blood has drenched Kali's temple and washed over the idol, the head is severed and the tail is placed—like so—between his teeth." He inserts an index finger in Lorna's gaping mouth. "Each head is laid before the idol"—he drops dramatically on his knees, pantomimes setting this grizzly burden down—"peaceful. It's—it's intimate, you see? Perfect." The black eyes have not left her once. "Kali is satiated. Until once again she rides out into the universe to play astride her consort, wreaking her lovely destruction."

S–Stella? Lorna motions desperately with her eyes.

Stella peels the headphones back until they flop around her neck. *"Big Chill,"* she says. "Great stuff."

Lorna looks straight at Stella. She must alert Stella without letting the man know. They must get out of here. Very slowly she says, "Apparently Kali's underrated." Stella mock-frowns then shrieks with laughter. "HEEE! Not my problem." Then slips the headphones back over her ears.

The man removes the pipe from between his teeth, levers the bowl against his outstretched thumb. Suddenly he flings his hand toward the trees. "That your car back there?"

"Yes," Lorna says then thinks she shouldn't have replied.

"In Dasain we pour blood over cars, trucks, anything that moves, to gain protection for the coming year." The man flips back his forelock. "You sure that thing is safe? I wouldn't want anything unpleasant to happen to you girls." Then he begins to laugh soundlessly, his head thrown back. An imitation of laughter. His throat looks pale, private.

Lorna has made a decision. She will ignore him. Pretend he's not there. Stella, after all, doesn't seem to know or care. It's the heat, the sun that's doing this to her. The crawling in her neck is just her fever, a chill. Lorna plucks the guidebook from where she left it earlier on the bench. If she just focuses her mind on something, this hallucination will disappear. She reads: "'On the ninth day of Dasain, tools, implements and all other mechanical devices must not be used. For the male manifestation of Kali or Durga, called Vishwa Karma, must be propitiated then. Tools, military weapons and hunters' knives are laid out under a carpet of flowers, incense and burning candles in honor of the Great Carpenter. A duck is brought up to the puja site, squawking, or sometimes a bleating goat. The animal is given food, sprinkled with holy water, then a magic phrase is whispered in its ear. Now it is up to the deity to give a signal. If the animal shakes its body, nods its head or flicks its ear, the god has entered its body and given consent to be sacrificed. The tools, implements, including students' books, doctors' instruments and other professional tools, are then drenched with the sacrificial blood. If the animal shows no sign, it has been rejected by the deity and allowed to live. Another goat or duck is quickly offered in its place. Vehicles also are safeguarded in this way.'"

Lorna closes the book and sets it down beside her, accidentally knocking the man's foot. Skin pops over muscle in his forearm. He presses a balled fist against his thigh, releases it slowly, deliberately, making sure Lorna sees. To Stella,

Lorna says, "Personally I like Shiva, the bull. How about you?" She is joking, trying to pull Stella with her into common memory, the self-styled guide at Pashupati temple who predicted dire consequences when they refused to worship the lingam, the fat stone phallus representing Shiva. But Stella doesn't hear.

Instead the stranger pulls the pipe out of his mouth and lifts his head back the same way as before—not too far. An imitation of his imitation. Lorna catches sight of teeth chiseled separate by decay.

"Oh, Lord," says Stella. Lorna turns her head, follows Stella's gaze. Beside the stone altar, a man struggles with the rope collar of his goat. The goat squirms. The other men, the blood-covered one they saw earlier, and a helper also stand by the goat. The three of them chat and joke. And then the goat is on its knees. The throat spurts and thickens. A knife flashes above the idol, which runs crimson.

On impulse Lorna looks behind her. The man with the pipe is gone.

They drive home the way they came. "Cheer up," says Stella and pulls what looks like a piece of dirty string from her purse. "Here, I meant to show you these before." She hands Lorna a pair of silver meditation bells.

"They blacken the string to make them look old," says Stella. She takes out a small wooden hammer and taps them into a ringing vortex of sound.

"Oh, Stella!"

"Hnnnnnnn . . . " Stella hands Lorna the mallet. "I got them in Ladakh from Seymour."

"Seymour?" Stella doesn't answer right away. The curves here are tight and deep. "American, hnnnnnnn . . . dentist. Okay, so what? He's been in Asia about as long as you've been alive, and he took me to this Buddhist retreat. Gawd! I thought that ascetic stuff died in the sixties. Next door to torture, but I stuck it out. Not sleeping, not eating, not talking. . . . A lot of walking, though, back and forth in this tiny courtyard. Ants on a postage stamp. Locals wandering around in purple robes and funky hats. The usual four-legged creatures everywhere. Canines came in from town around eleven." Stella jerks her foot off the gas. "Oops, watch out for that shit pile! My guru (you get a guru) was the silent but deep type. . . . Looked a lot like Stevie Wonder. Dogs howled till three in the morning. Then the hawking and spitting on the men's side something terrible. That started around four. So you can imagine the major impetus to get up, at five mind you, is a violent urge to vomit."

Lorna taps the bells, one, two, in quick succession. Stella glances at her, but Lorna pretends not to notice. She pretends to be floating inside sound.

"The better you get at meditation," says Stella, "the more you clear your head of all the mundane worries. I'm only at the novice level, but Seymour's at a higher one."

Lorna tries to picture Stella and Seymour walking, meditating in the postage-stamp courtyard. Did they talk, touch? Did they notice each other in the normal way, perhaps through a kind of haze—or at all?

"It's really a spiritual brother-sister sort of thing with Seymour," says Stella. "He's very deep." Lorna can see Stella is serious.

"I'm serious, Lo, I'm the first woman Seymour's made love to in eight years. He said he's been practising celibacy for ten, but the first two got a bit screwed up. But he's reached a plane now where sex is okay as long as it's done properly. Well not the actual way. I mean—it has to do with purity and ecstatic apprehension of God. Like, take for example the first time we made love. Gawd! He shows me one of those statues, you know, with Shiva and Parvati going at it, except this one, no kidding, is pure gold! He said he'd had it made specially. . . . Anyway, we're sitting—fully clothed, Lorna—on his floor, well, in the hotel, cross-legged, and he puts this statue between us."

"Hold it! You mean he lugs this thing around with him, or does he live in the hotel?"

"It's only a small statue, Lo, a figurine I guess you'd call it. He puts it between us and then closes his eyes and starts to meditate. At least I guess that's what he's doing, so I do, too. It was hard to pick up at first. By this time, Lo, I'm on fire. I can't think of anything but his cock. After what seems like a decent length of time, I sneak a peek to see if he's got big yet. Lo, his eyes are wide open, he's staring straight at me. I was mortified. He said I wasn't ready yet, but for being a good sport we could lie naked together. And that's what we did. Finito. I learned pretty fast after that. Hnnnnnnn . . . but even so, he'll only make love at certain times. Something to do with the moon. And then afterward he won't have anything but boiled water for three days."

Stella gears down, third, then second. The engine has been lugging since she jumped the gas. The hill they are on must be steeper than it looks. Lorna glances in the side mirror on her door. Behind them a jeep, the first vehicle they have seen since Daxinkali, is gaining on them more quickly than Lorna would have thought possible given the slope they are climbing. She looks at Stella.

"You see that guy?"

"Hmmm?" Stella says. "This damn piece of junk. What's happened to the power?"

In the rearview mirror, the jeep is catching up.

"What's wrong? Just floor it, Stell. Pedal to the metal—only way to go in this country."

Stella looks at her. Lorna notices one of Stella's eyebrows is slightly higher than the other.

"What're you doing now?"

Stella pulls over by a depression in the road. "You wanna drive?"

"No, no, it's okay," Lorna says, although she does. The jeep rolls up behind them and stops. The man from Daxinkali swings down from his seat. Lorna feels feverish again.

"C'mon, we should be getting—"

"—give it a rest! We're overheating."

"Oh—oh. I didn't know—"

Stella rolls her eyes, which in turn pull her head away. She stares out her window across the road. "Goddamn country. . . ." She mumbles and wrenches the window open.

The man walks up toward them. Something is hanging from his belt Lorna hasn't noticed before, a leather sheath.

"Christ! It's an oven—" Stella winds the window further down.

The man already has his head in Stella's window when Lorna starts to think about the jeep. She doesn't remember seeing it at Daxinkali. His face quickens, grins over Stella's turned head. His teeth, what's left of them, are yellow. Nicotine, she thinks. To Lorna the body is a temple.

"Miss?" he say, looking at Lorna.

"Uh . . . uh, yes." Lorna glances at Stella stalled in some daydream "You forgot something." He reaches behind him and pulls out Stella's guidebook. It is too big to fit in a pocket. He must have had it stuffed down the back of his pants. He reaches across Stella and hands Lorna the book. His wrist is pale yet unusually thick for his otherwise slender body. He doesn't let go right away. The cover twists so the pages spread out in a fan. But his grip loosens suddenly, and Lorna's hand knocks painfully against the dash.

She starts to thank him, just a few words to complete her casual disguise. He raises his hand, lifts his lip in what might be a kind of sneer, as if she should know better, and walks away. Stella rolls up her window and slips the clutch. Lorna's eye follows the long legs' stride back to the jeep.

"Good riddance," she says. Stella doesn't seem to hear. Something beats in Lorna, a shiver of wings. Like the feeling before her period, but it's too early.

"You getting your period or something?" says Stella. Familiarity breaks along Lorna's memory—a recurring dream she has: skydiving, she forgets the parachute. "Maybe. I don't keep track." A lie. "Why?" she snaps, "Are you?"

Stella seems amused by the question. "Not bloody likely," she says. "I'd be getting on for menopause by now, I guess— that is if I had the parts." Lorna says nothing, stares at Stella, the soft down of her cheek.

"Man, ya had to be there," Stella is saying, "the-Pill-shall-make-you-free time, dig? I mean if you weren't popping 'em, you were counting 'em." *Dig.* The word spreading in Lorna's ears, stinging. Stella glances over at Lorna. "Ah, you're such a babe." She leans deep into a curve, brushes Lorna's arm with her own. "Anyway, 'So Stell,' I said to myself, 'be smart.' I got a coil." Stella laughs. "That's when I got fucked. Hnnnnnn ... it's like the song says—'Ya get what ya need.' Huh. PID."

"Pelvic Inflammatory Disease," says Lorna.

"'The Price of Sexual Permissiveness' is what the doctors called it. This is after they relieved me of my uterus."

"How do you feel about it now?"

"You sound like a shrink," says Stella. "I feel fine. No bloody periods, no rotten husbands or screaming kids. It's like the doctor said. I'm there after the operation, completely wasted in postop, crying my eyes out. 'What's the problem now?' he says. 'It's over! You should be happy!'" Stella shrugs her shoulders. "I'm happy."

The road begins to straighten, and Lorna rolls her window all the way down; she's eyeing a gully, watching for the river. After a while Stella says, "Look. It's no big deal. There're people starving in India, y'know? Hnnnnnnn . . . I mean, it's no one's fault. Karma, right? Mine's different from yours. The last thing I want at this point's a white fucking picket fence. Believe me." Just then the Toyota crests a hill. Lorna leans out of her window as far as she dares, but the gully drops away behind a steep bank.

Then, for the first time since the man handed it back, Lorna looks down at Stella's guidebook in her lap. It is different somehow, though the cover, the title, the size, the thickness are the same as before. The book looks as though it has sat in a musty bookstore for a decade or more. The bold clarity of the cover illustration—Durga-Kali dancing her dance of death, the demon-black body, her necklace of white skulls, scarlet blood dripping from her mouth—is subdued, darkened. It's as though the book's been through a muddy wash. The pages ripple slightly like they might have been thumbed over in a bath. Otherwise it is like new, not soiled or carelessly folded back.

"Let's see that." Stella holds out her hand. Lorna hands her the book. Stella reads out: "'On the tenth day, the climax of the Dasain celebration, Kathmandu swarms with people dressed up in their finest, rushing from one end of the Valley to the other, paying their respects to elder relatives from whom they receive *tika* blessing, a dot of vermilion powder mixed with rice and curd placed on the forehead by the elder's hand. There is a crush of last minute offerings made at Kali temples, too—' oops!" Stella, reading as she drives, steers them back on to the road, which they had nearly left. She continues: "'In the afternoon of that day, Buddhist priests, dressed up in costume as deities Kali, Bhairab, Kumari, Ganesh and others, dance in ecstasy through the streets, brandishing huge swords, symbols of Durga's power. When the heavy weapon begins to vibrate out of control in his hand, the priest has been completely possessed by the deity whose dress and mask he displays. Now and then, in hypnotic trance or ecstasy caused by day-long fasting, throbbing drums, burning incense and incantation, the masked deity lunges into the crowd. Everyone scatters in fear only to close around him again when the sword calms down. It is on this day that Lord Rama slew the demon Ravana to recapture his virtuous Sita, and, in response to the prayers of gods and men, mother Durga rode out in fury upon a lion to vanquish the evil buffalo demon Mahisa, restoring the world to good.'

Hmmm!" says Stella, "whadayaknow?"

By the time they see the traffic jam on Bagmati Bridge, it is too late to avoid it. Stella pulls among the honking Tata trucks, buses, bicycles, rickshaws, jeeps and taxis. They wait. After a minute or so, Stella gets out. Lorna watches her push expertly through the crowd.

That is when she sees him—an instant carved on pipe and cheekbone, black hair more pronounced for his white skin. Lorna snaps forward, strains to find him again. But her eyes have become prisms, deflecting sight.

Stella returns, flops back in her seat. "Someone hit a cow," she says. "Poor bugger." By this she means the penalty is the same as for manslaughter. That's if you were lucky, and the police got there before the mob.

Stella turns off the motor. "Well," she says, "when all else fails, read the directions." She yanks a dusty tourist pamphlet from the side pocket on her door and pretends to read: "What to do when caught in a nauseating traffic jam on Bagmati Bridge at rush hour. One: find the cause of the hold up. Check. Two: if it is anything but an injured or dead cow, stay calm. It will clear up shortly. If it is an injured or dead cow, see Three. Three: determine whether you are the cause. If you are, see Four. Four: do not stop. Do not pass Go. Drive home, remove your license plates and paint your car black. Walk for at least three weeks."

Lorna laughs. "Let me see that." She reads: *"Bagmati* comes from two words—*bagnu,* meaning to flow, and *mati,* wisdom or understanding. The Bagmati River, which divides Patan from Kathmandu, flows south through the Chobar Gorge and drains into the Great Gangetic Plain of India.' The flow of understanding. I like that." She didn't bring a purse, so tucks the pamphlet in Stella's. "Remind me to get it later, okay?"

Stella pushes open her door and stands up. Lorna unlocks hers, makes her way around the front of the car to Stella. The sun is falling in a pink blaze behind Nagarjun.

"By the way, the pamphlet's wrong."

"Huh?"

"All that stuff about bagnu and matu or whatever," Stella says. "A local I picked up the other day says it's wrong. He said it's really an adulteration of—I forget—a goddess or priestess or something. Whoever wrote that thing was out to lunch. Jesus, it's dark already."

Hard to get used to, this quick absence between light and dark. It is new moon; the first clouds of monsoon are rolling over the valley, blotting out the stars. Lorna and Stella lean over the bridge, peering into yawning blackness where the river should be.

"What they need here is a revolution . . ." Stella says.

"Shhh, Stella." There is a police patrol post at the other end of the bridge; Lorna can see two of them inside playing dice by a kerosene lantern.

". . . of the Thomas Edison variety. Hnnnnnnn . . ."

A pinprick of light appears in the water. Lorna looks up. On the roof of Thapatali Maternity Hospital, at the foot of the statue of a mother holding a child in her arms, someone is fixing a spotlight.

"Hey, Stella, look at Hail Mary in a Sari!" Stella's name for the statue.

But Stella has disappeared into the car. A smell, strong and sour, bores through Lorna's nostrils, lodges behind her eyes.

By the time Lorna rejoins Stella in the car, a human river is breaking around them, surging toward the cow, trying to get close enough to touch it. Some beleaguered-looking men struggle to lift the animal onto a wooden cart, but the press of bodies prevents them.

Lorna feels the car begin to rock; she and Stella are jostled in their seats. Then a thump; the car shakes. Something bangs on the trunk, and . . . no, it's not possible. . . . The Toyota slides backward a little. More. Why doesn't Stella start the engine?

Lorna turns to Stella. Stella *is* driving—forward. This is what tricked her: they were moving in, but slower than, the current. Ahead, the human confluence is steadily receding. Near Lorna's window, a woman stops and dips her hand reverently in the blood on the pavement, then touches her forehead.

The acrid smell makes Lorna's head ache. More than ache. Her skull seems to shrink against her brain. She wipes her eyes of heat. How much further to Stella's hotel? Lorna has never come into town this way before.

Then they are there. HOTEL BLUE STAR. Behind the sign, the hotel garden is tranquil. Down the road, at this end of Bagmati Bridge, the little police hut glows.

"Blue Star, Blue Star here we come!" sings Stella. "Right back where we started from!" As they snap to a halt, Lorna grabs for the broken seat belt dangling beside her—too late. With the other hand, she breaks her fall against the dash.

"You're coming, aren't you?" Stella says climbing out.

"Yes, yes, of course," Lorna says, then realizes Stella means to her room.

"Good," says Stella. "I've got some smuggled wine and stuff. Gotta get while the getting's good, as they say! Gonna show us girls some good times!"

"You're jolly."

Stella says something, but Lorna doesn't hear. Through the window, in the lobby—but he's already disappeared. When they go in, sudden blackness, confusion. The power has failed again.

"Gawd!" Stella's voice in the dark. Then silence. "They never heard of candles in this country?"

Something brushes against Lorna, moving air. She sniffs the darkness. A pipe? Or does she just imagine. . . . A candle floats toward them, then another. One by one tiny flames skitter into view, reluctant stars composing constellations. Lorna's eyes press the dimness. He is here somewhere, she can feel it.

"Coming?" Stella grabs a candle from RESEPTION, leads Lorna up the stairs.

In her room Stella suddenly slows down. Candle by candle she lights a large brass candelabra, as though the act were more important than its result. Now the room seems to blaze with light, and Lorna looks around.

"How long do you figure you'll be here?" Lorna indicates the room, festooned with the paraphernalia of Stella's lovers' loves—miniature dirigibles floating above tiny waving teddy bears, tarnished but serenely seated Buddhas, photographs of light patterns through tatami mats (the last signed, "Hiko – Japan.")

Stella eases down on the bed, rolls onto her back. "Few days, I guess. Hey, listen, you look awful." She pats the bed. Lorna flops down next to Stella and lies back.

"Oh, Stella, everything hurts."

"I thought you might say that. Hnnnnnnn . . . hey, you want some tea?" Stella points to a kettle across the room on the window ledge. "I got the kettle on the black market in some ridiculous little country way back when."

"No thanks, I'm too tired."

They lie side by side without speaking for a long time. Lorna thinks about mentioning the wine. Why not? Stella offered. But it's not polite. She's a guest after all, this is Stella's room. But aren't they better friends than that? Lorna stares at the candle flames, separate and still, as if the air in this room never moved at all.

"You don't need to do that, you know," Lorna says, her voice an odd shape in the hush. She did not know she was going to speak.

"Do what?"

"Get kettles—and things—on the black market."

"What are you talking about?"

"You can go down to Asan Tole, go to the Supermarket and buy them at Western prices like everyone else."

"What? Suddenly we're little Miss Conscience? Miss Morality of 1986? Half that stuff's illegal anyway. No one buys it. They're just ripping you off."

Maybe it's true after all. Maybe they are ripping you off. What exactly had she meant? Lorna wishes now she'd never brought it up. Stella gets up from the bed, leans against a creaky wooden table and from somewhere in the darkness pulls out a cigarette.

"I didn't know you smoked."

"You don't know, you don't know. You don't like this, you don't like that."

Lorna can see Stella's hand shake, holding the cigarette. Stella lays the cigarette back down on the table and picks up an enormous authentic-looking kukhri knife. She pulls it from its brass-studded black leather sheath. "You always hold the back of the sheath . . . like this," she says. "That way you don't cut yourself in the event the knife slices the sheath open." Lorna wonders where Stella got the deadly weapon but no longer feels compelled to ask. Stella runs a finger along the curved razor edge of the long blade.

"Maybe I should go home," Lorna says.

Stella drops the knife against her thigh. "And maybe I should go to Thailand. It's my next country. I've got an open ticket."

"Oh, Stella." Lorna sits up, pulls herself back against the wall. But the words are just habit now. Lorna doesn't feel them at all.

Stella lifts the knife and spits or pretends to spit on the blade. She begins to run a finger up and down.

"There's nothing you've seen in this world, my dear, that poor bitter Stella hasn't seen first. Yes, why don't you go home. You're a married woman after all. What about the Incredible Hunk?" Stella's name for John. Stella turns on her radio voice. "Hey, Hunks out there, do you know where your wife is?"

As she speaks, smoke rings halo Stella's head. She hasn't yet lit the cigarette. Lorna starts but knows better than to let on. Without a word she leaves the bed, traverses the thick room to the door. She slips out—Stella watching—and brings it gently to.

Downstairs in the lobby, the night clerk winks her past the sleeping doorman. "Too late going." Standing behind his desk in the glass. "Too" meaning "very." Very late, not too. Through his bloodshot eye, Lorna reaches for her reflection.

KICHIKINNY

Some sleep better—dreamless—beneath a pillow. But Lorna dreams. Something touches her face. Pencil, charcoal, small knife scraping skin. Thick lines, circles, swirls—the nose looks different, straighter; the mouth, wider; cheeks—Sometime in the night, Lorna returns. The face she finds, not her own. Somewhere an eyelash roars against a pillow.

In the dark he had reached out. In her sleep. And she, in sleep, recoiled. Sleepless now, pale skin in the window, face unfamiliar.

Downstairs in the lobby, the night clerk winks her past the sleeping doorman. "Too late going." Standing behind his desk in the glass. "Too" meaning "very." Very late, not too. Through his bloodshot eye, Lorna reaches for her reflection.

Up through the tiny hotel garden. Lorna peers over the low picket gate into the street. The darkness to her left: Kopundol hill and Patan, the old city. The darkness to her right falls down to Bagmati River and the bridge. Behind darkness more darkness rising: Kathmandu, home. Lorna slips the latch of the little wooden gate, thinks for an instant of a long-ago latch, a cottage on another planet. She steps out.

The road has disappeared. In its place a tunnel thickens under high walls rimmed with broken glass. She reaches quickly back for the wooden gate. Pricks her finger instead on the tall thorn hedge that has grown up in its place. An intensity of blackness seems to press down. She must go on alone in darkness between these long walls toward home. She remembers such a wall growing up around her home; at the time she paid no attention. Laughed when Vishnu, the chaukidar, piled brick on brick, calling the wall protection. From thieves, pariah dogs, he said, and ghosts, in which Lorna does not believe.

White pant legs flicker on her eye rims as she moves. Her feet glide, soundless, thieves under a thieves' moon. Hands not her own sway invisibly by her sides. Once, fingers brush her leg and Lorna jumps. Is she invisible? But the white pants blink again, undenied. Lorna glances to either side, looks for openings, a gate. There are one or two—high, iron-barred, padlocked. A dog pokes out its muzzle and growls, a long whine backing slowly down its throat.

A shadow in the gloom ahead draws nearer. The shape slides and changes, becomes a familiar temple to which, in the daylight, she has traveled. But now no colorful worshippers adorn the idols, no monkeys laugh, no children play among the gods. Only the stone lingum, phallic symbol of Shiva, rises in the night to meet her. Something is wrong, backward. The temple should be on her right side, not her left. Despite a lingering sweetness in the air—incense?—Lorna looks away, passes by quickly. Soon she should be coming to the river.

Breath congeals, eyes tighten on the darkness. If only she could see Bagmati Bridge. But nothing climbs out of the blackness except the sheen of road ahead. Is there a small rise in the downward-curving street? She can't remember. Everything is backward on this road. When she faces downhill toward the Bagmati River and the bridge, Lorna begins to climb. When she turns back up the hill to the old city-kingdom of Patan and the Hotel Narayan, her feet reverse direction down to the bridge.

Something gleams in the distance. The river! Lorna hurries ahead, barely mindful of her mounting feet. Then stops. A sound: clean and quiet. *Tick, tick*—slow footsteps coming toward her. And under the steps, a steady beat, dull thudding, she now realizes she's been hearing for some time. She makes out the white belt and shined boots of an army patrol beating a long nightstick on his fist. The fingers, one ear and the tip of his nose are strangely luminous, but Lorna cannot see a source of light.

When the white first flickered on his vision, Hari pulled his lathi from his belt. It was difficult to say whether the specter moved toward him or away. Night played tricks on the eyes, he knew. Before it appeared Hari had been dozing, daydreaming a little of his new baby daughter. A son would have been preferable, of course, but he and Gita had time. He had even heard of a doctor in New Road who could alter the sex of the fetus. These days, all in all, Hari felt a lucky man. Their daughter was quite healthy and beautiful, and they could all live reasonably on his wage. Yes, Hari thought, Shiva has not been unkind.

Then this white color flickering on the night. Closer . . . closer . . . until, level with his patrol hut, the vision scissors in two: a pair of loose trousers, walking. But who would come here at this hour, long after curfew? It is a habit of Hari to tap his lathi on the palm of his hand. He is doing that now as he steps from the sidewalk and strolls into the road. What he sees there stops him dead. Oh, Krishna! What has heaven sent?

"K'a jau?"

Her cheeks rise wide, high into her eyes; her tongue pokes for an instant between fine teeth. "Dheramaa jaane."

Something pulls Hari's eye downward, a bit of shoulder bone exposed by the loose shirt near her throat. The lathi begins its tapping again in Hari's hand. "K'a gayo?"

She points the wrong way down the road. "Patan gaeko."

Is this memsahib playing with him, maybe flirting a little? Something glints in Hari's head. A story he heard as a child and later, too, of a woman who comes out after dark. . . .

"K'a bas'?"

She points back to Patan. "Kathmandu. Bisal Nagarmaa baschhu."

What language is she speaking? It is not like tourist language that comes out the nose. The sounds this creature makes are right, but the words are stiff and slow. They are too long and careful, too complete, as if she's standing on a street in another world beside this one, deliberately making the right noises wrong. And Hari's never heard of this district she claims to live in. Not anyway in Kathmandu. Well, steady predictable Hari can play this game, too.

"Kas'ri jau, *taxi*maa 'ina?" He opens his mouth in a wide grin on "taxi," like a tourist-sahib talking through his nose. "M'laai *dherai taxi* m'np'rchha. Tim'lai ni? Taxi *dherai ramre* chha!"

But she doesn't seem to get the joke. You'd think he rode in taxis every day, the way she takes for granted his comment about liking them. Her chin rises a little at the word *taxi*, that's all. Then another odd string of words comes out, ancient sounding, as though they were dug up from the ground. Something about a house, an hour—the words are clear as anything, but still Hari cannot understand. Perhaps, after all, she's just a fine lady from another world who lost her way in this one. Or—

Hari has a thought that makes his lathi jump—was she between worlds? Now the elders' story comes flooding back. Sometimes it happened that a whore or nymphomaniac escaped complete cremation. Her soul would then go wandering, reincarnated as the dreaded kichikinny, a ghost-woman who roamed the streets at night, hunting men down, seducing them, dragging them off to some lonely place. . . . It feels like he's been punched, though Hari's sure nothing's touched him. His head floats, his belly feels ice cold. But only for a minute. He must remember who he is. What kind of soldier faints away before a woman, a memsahib at that? Now Hari becomes serious. All joking about taxis aside, Hari points out his hut. She should wait there.

She doesn't move that way. Instead she comes a little nearer. He can see a dark bulge rounding out her blouse. For a breast it seems huge, but it could just be a shadow. Then her teeth flash against darkness, and her strange mouth opens up to speak. This time even the words are unfamiliar—the sounds unrecognizable except as some vague utterance out of a long-ago dream.

She should have pretended not to understand. But she keeps her hand out, pointing far into the darkness where she thinks home is. The soldier does not look where she is pointing but slaps the nightstick hard against his wrist. Which way is she heading? Which has she come from? He is teasing her, of course, asking where she's been. Somehow he already knows. The soldier points his nightstick down the road before her. Lorna's stomach rises, her knees twist.

"K'a gayo?"

She points after his nightstick down the road. "Patan gaeko." The man pulls back then, offended, Lorna thinks, or angry.

"K'a bas' nuh?"

Lorna has to separate the tight words in her head. She tells him where she lives, a newer district on the city's northern fringe. But she should not have told the truth. It's too far, he won't believe her, already she sees that.

"Taxi" is the single word she snags in his next fury. Lorna laughs high—taxis have long since quit for the night. Something trickles along her scalp. "Dheramaa pharkane laageko ek ghanTaa—" No, all wrong, her words, their order and tenses, wrong. To get home, she tried to say, it would only take an hour. Does the soldier smile? Lorna becomes conscious of being braless, feels her nipples touch the thin fabric of her husband's shirt, which she wears tied in a knot around her waist. "Hour"—it meant, "ek ghanTaa"—one hour. What has she said?

A deep bitter smell, like cardamom. He's moved in again, blocking her way. "Taxi . . . taxi!"—words stabbing air. Why does he smile so on the word *taxi*? Why this silly talk of liking taxis very much, and did she, too? He jerks his head toward his hut, a little shack set back from the street. Lorna can see the orange glow of a kerosene lantern through a crack. Her throat burns, tears and fear and fatigue demanding indulgence but forced back. That thumping. The nightstick beating now in her chest. The skin of her upper arm buzzes and buzzes, foretelling the weight of his grip—

—how the kichikinny is said to be very beautiful but unable to speak properly, only yelp like a monkey. She is known to be sadistic, torturing men to death by tickling, screaming with pleasure at the doomed men's giggling. The she-monster could be recognized, though, if a man knew the signs: enormous swinging breasts and feet that were reversed toe to heel. Hari wants to look down and check; for this he must dare take his eyes from her face. But her feet are invisible in the dark, below the strange luminous pantaloons, which themselves might conceal a weapon.

When his eyes start to wander down her body, Lorna steps out. Her ears roar. Her limbs feel useless and separate from her, as though she were caught in a flood. "Excuse me, I really must go home now," she says loudly in English to drown the nightmare out. For a long time, walking at top speed, Lorna will not look back. Her ears ache with fear—a shout? Boots ticking behind her? Her thigh muscles twitch with impatience—to go faster, to run. But she will not lose control. Finally, her feet racing forward beneath her, Lorna dares turn her head. The white-belted khaki uniform sprints in long, long strides back to the shack. There he will get his partner, alert every patrol post along her way. Now she can no longer hold back. A dog growls from a garbage heap beside her and, whimpering, Lorna breaks into a run.

Hari slumps on the single wooden bench in the shack, his head in shaking hands. Some way down the road, she looked back, as the kichikinny is said to do, trying to get a man to follow. In the story a group of friends thinks to vanquish the roving kichikinny. But when they ambush her, only one, the bravest, dares. For the man who seeks to overcome the man-hungry ghost-woman must throw his arms around her quickly and hold her still until dawn. How close he had come! She might have lured him, too, had he not remembered the stories and got away. Hari thinks about his mother, getting older now and needing more attention, and Gita, a good wife, shy and pretty enough and obedient to his mother's increasing demands. He thinks Shiva is sending him a message. Hari has a bad feeling in the pit of his stomach. He aches for night to be over and his shift with it so that he can get home to Gita's soft hands massaging his feet, his calves, his thighs. . . . Hari closes his eyes and dreams the courtyard of their apartment is a green open meadow with a clear stream babbling through and gentle large-eyed does romping across, feeding on enormous orange flowers.

VISHNU'S DREAM

It's all written ahead of time by the gods, all that will ever happen. When I die, I won't tell you.
—*Vishnu Maya Gurung*

Her belly warm and full, her body stone tired, chanting the gods' names to herself, the old widow Vishnu Maya drew the blanket up over her. The long list of names came to her tongue without fail every morning and night, although in the daytime she couldn't think of one if you asked her. But they fell out of her mouth, even tonight, when her head clattered with darshan, this pilgrimage she was making with her sister: YE ISWAR VISHNU BHAGWAN VISHNU JAGGANATH PASHUPATINATH SWYAMBUNATH MUKTINATH....

First they caught a bus to Kathmandu city. On the way a young woman died. Her friends handed her out through the window into a forest of arms, then pushed down the middle of the bus themselves to the door. It took all day to get to Kathmandu, up and down, and they still had a long walk to Pashupatinath temple from where the bus stopped. Still Vishnu Maya felt like dancing in the noisy rancid streets. Dancing the way she and a friend had danced when they were girls, keeping in step while blindfolded, dancing for the other villagers who would laugh when either went out of step—*ghaanto* dancers.

She and Gauri, alone together in Kathmandu, untethered from the daily chores. Sure they were homesick at first. But they fixed their minds on their devotions and on the words of the priests and others they talked with at Pashupatinath, Jagganath, Swyambunath, Budhanilkantha, all the Hindu and Buddhist centers of worship. They met a woman at Swyambunath who had run away from her home in the hills with a soldier who then left her for a city girl half his age. The three —Vishnu Maya, Gauri and the young woman—sat smoking on the cobbled courtyard beneath Buddha's huge eyes and joked together like teenagers: "Why take this man's cigarette when another one offered a cigar! *Kyaak! Kyaak!*" The young woman's laugh was like an axe biting wood.

Then all three of them walked up a long hill to Budhanilkantha, where the great god Vishnu lay sleeping, blue and prone, among the snake's coils in the sacred water, dreaming the world. Vishnu Maya thought a lot about this dream. When her back felt like a plank of wood after planting or her no-good son-in-law stumbled drunk across her doorstep asking for money, Vishnu Maya thought about what a Brahmin once told her—that everything around her, her own life, was just a dream, Vishnu's dream. When Vishnu Maya had protested—"Is this brick not here by my foot, do you not see it, too?"—the Brahmin said, "Yes, I see it, everyone does, we're all in the same dream."

After Budhanilkantha, Vishnu Maya and Gauri got tired of the city, the hard cement floors and paved roads under their feet, and took a bus back to the hills. From there they would begin the long journey to the holy shrine of Muktinath, the goal of their pilgrimage. *Muktinath.* The name had glittered twice a day on Vishnu Maya's tongue for as long as she could remember. *Muktinath.* The very word promised release from the endless weary circle of sow and reap, day and night.

So they started north. Ahead an ever-steepening wall of frozen waves. Green familiar hills rolled upward from the sisters' feet to the horizon. Then, as they rose to its crest, that horizon receded and changed. Always they returned, though, to a valley's cool shade and the river they had lived beside all their lives. Whenever Vishnu Maya caught sight of that river, something moved in her chest and belly as though the world's rum spirits all poured in at once. How must the river feel, then, for the nagas, serpent spirits that controlled the water's flow and purity, were always swimming up and down the river's cool depths. The wriggling nagas would be delicious, warm along the river's belly. That is why she rushed and rolled and squirmed between the hills—for sheer pleasure!

For nearly eighty years this river had fed Vishnu Maya. And now she was walking to its source. "Muktinath," she said out loud, still not quite believing. "Muktinath," Gauri repeated. "Muktinath," Vishnu Maya incanted. And the word brought its own satisfaction.

Up, up, up—*the world is more like a tree than a paddy field,* mused Vishnu Maya. *You are always either climbing, branching off or descending. And, indeed, terrace fields are not God-given; we cut them out of these hills with our hands.* Even the path they walked on was worn in places to the depth of a man's height—like walking through a burning tunnel into the earth.

At Taatopaani they bathed in the hot pool of water, clutching their skirts around the tops of their old breasts, baring their shoulders to the soothing heat. Vishnu Maya felt her calves ease a little; her thighs and her back flesh, wound up tighter than a chicken's neck before the snap, softened under the hot liquid hands. Sweat jeweled the white hairs at the top of her forehead. One large bead slid down the brown cheek near her mouth. The warm water lapped the deep corduroy of her cheeks, found some half-forgotten ache and drew it out. Her skin smoothed down, like the air after a monsoon storm. A cloud drifted in her ear, vaporized thought. *What relief to think of nothing,* Vishnu Maya thought! *But I am thinking about thinking about nothing, and so I am thinking about something after all.* She was enjoying this conversation in her head and was just sitting back to hear it continue, when some words spoke out loud in her head. The mantra she'd chanted in India those years ago. But the mantra refused to hop onto her tongue. When she tried to find it again, the syllables vanished in the steam, collapsed, then left her completely. "Come out of there," Gauri said from the edge of the pool. "Are you hoping to fool Bhagwan into thinking you're a raisin?" Vishnu Maya tried ignoring her, slid down a little deeper till the damp hairs in her nostrils barely quivered above the water. She tried thinking about nothing again, but now she could only think of the sharp stone digging in the back of her thigh. And the soles of her feet were stinging, too. The spices in this water must be strong, strong enough perhaps to soak through the skin and shrivel someone up inside. Vishnu Maya reached her hand up and, with Gauri's help, climbed out of the pool.

Up, up, up. Their thick soles cracking deeper. She and Gauri gripped their ankles and laughed—their footpads looked like the mud bottom of a dry creek. Vishnu Maya reached into her sack and felt around for the bottle of rum. Gauri said, "Just put it on my feet."

"These spirits work better inside," said Vishnu Maya. And tipped the bottle to her mouth. Right away she felt them swimming down her chest under her skin. She offered some to Gauri, who refused. So Vishnu Maya poured some more in for luck, tucked the bottle away and led off again up the trail. But the pains in her feet and back were not eased for long. Step by slow step, Vishnu Maya pulled herself up the steep trail. She could feel the blood boil in her thighs, calves and feet, like too-long-forgotten tea water. Her ears popped with steam.

The trail led down again to a partly dried riverbed, then disappeared in the boulders and rounded rocks. She and Gauri diverted each other by pointing out and collecting magic stones. They knew certain rocks along this part of the river were used by lamas to bring rain, but neither sister was sure which ones. As the day drew on, the sisters' feet slipped off the rocks, their ankle bones were pummeled and bruised. Vishnu Maya prayed to the rum spirits. *Swim!* she prayed, and waited for their cool trickle down her limbs. But the spirits had gone to sleep.

The word rose suddenly, molded her breath before she knew. *Muktinath. Muktinath.* Vishnu Maya chanted the sacred name over and over now. Perhaps Muktinath would take her mind off her feet. When you couldn't go to the gods, sometimes they would come to you. She loved to hear the name roll from her tongue. But the more she intoned the sacred name, the more it seemed to say, "Sore knees and feet." *Sometimes up on their mountains,* she thought, *even the gods play jokes and dice.* Vishnu Maya rumbled the magic stones in her hand, looked up at Gauri, who was far ahead. And in that moment, her legs flooded with relief.

Further up they came to a bridge made of nothing but rope loops joined by free-lying planks of wood. Vishnu Maya found Gauri waiting for her to cross first. When she did Gauri grabbed on to Vishnu Maya's bag from behind and refused to let go until they got to the other side. Here the trail followed a snake bend in the river. Vishnu Maya knew there would soon be another bridge. She knew Gauri still half-believed an old tale their father told them, that such bridges were the haunts of evil spirits. Vishnu Maya herself had overheard their father laugh over this clever story. But even now, when she knew it had been just a trick to keep small children from playing near water, Vishnu Maya half-believed it herself.

When they came to the bridge, a group of local women was about to cross toward them. Vishnu Maya and Gauri stopped to let them go first, but the group, seeing the pilgrims, told them to cross. "We'd better go fast," Vishnu Maya said to Gauri, "or the spirits will catch us!" Gauri's eyes grew round, and her hand reached automatically for her sister. But Vishnu Maya was already running ahead so Gauri couldn't catch her. The bridge swayed and snapped out of rhythm with Gauri's steps. Surely the bridge demons were after her now! Gauri spun around, dashed back the other way to the only thorn bush she could see and squatted down. Her father always said this was the best protection. "Ha! Ha!" laughed the women. Vishnu Maya, too, slapped her sides. Even Gauri grinned from behind the safety of the bush spines. "Do you see some evil spirits?" Vishnu Maya teased. She was laughing hard enough to burst. Then the group of women started across. Together they walked slowly up the step to the swinging bridge. Then, inflated by giggles and whispers, flew over to Gauri's side. That night in the bhatti, Gauri said, "It's true—evil spirits lurk around bridges."

Vishnu Maya said, "Those women were just making fun of you." Their hostess said nothing but stirred and stirred a kind of yellow mush.

They choked the unappetizing gruel down and listened to the woman's talk. She boasted that her tribe were kings of the Tibetan salt trade, hard currency for many generations back. Vishnu Maya was shocked to learn about an old tradition here—conscripting house servants and farm workers from poorer border tribes living to the north. Between the woman's words, Vishnu Maya saw how, receiving only grain as wages, the workers soon found themselves bond servants, hooked to their overlords—aggressive moneylenders—like fish on a line, slaving to pay off their debts. Vishnu Maya thought how different things were with her sharecroppers back home, a family of the low blacksmith caste. They were supposed to work her fields and bring one-half the harvested unthreshed grain and straw up from the field to her house. But they never worked as hard as they would on their own fields, and they didn't bring her all they should. These sharecroppers were clever. All season long they would complain about how poor the rice stand looked so they would be justified when Vishnu Maya's "half" looked suspiciously small.

She and Gauri came to a village that was the heart of the world. The sun licked the great flanks of Dhauligiri and Annapurna high above them, then swallowed its own light. To Vishnu Maya and her sister down on the trail, it was like walking into the dark mouth of God. Vishnu Maya remembered years ago walking for two days before an eclipse with her husband and some other villagers to a holy river. Everything around them got dark, and together they walked into the cold river and bathed. For the growth of one's karma, it was one of the best things you could do. But this village, Vishnu Maya could see, knew more about darkness than light. Everyone told her and Gauri to look backward the way they had come; they pointed out the silver tips of the mountains, the homes of the gods, the beautiful view. Gauri even wanted to stop for a snack where they could still watch the pink gods fly off the mountaintops into the clouds for the night. But here in the blackness between the mountains, Vishnu Maya lost interest in views. She clamped her hands on the straps of her head sack, shoved forward in its pull. "It's not nighttime yet," she said angrily. "There's more darkness ahead than that."

In the dark village, the whispering had started up in her ears. The bad spirits had come back. Angry spirits, who twisted around inside her, then disappeared, leaving her beaten up and flattened, like cornstalks after a hailstorm. Vishnu Maya quickened her pace, tried to outdistance the demons who shouted louder now, dampening the friendly rhythm of cowbells and faraway laughter. Now Gauri speeded up behind her sister. *Vishnu Maya looked a little like a buffalo,* she thought, *straining at its yoke.* The spirits sucked Vishnu Maya's brains into a hole. They screamed about revenge, what was wrong and right. "That Raam's wife," they said, "who lives at the bottom of your village, is her husband a colonel or lieutenant? While your dead husband was a fine colonel. But you can't wear good shoes to the bazaar and for woodcutting in the forest, like Raam's wife. And how about your cousin, Parbati? Is her husband so much as a sergeant? But she is always flaunting expensive clothes and gold bangles, even a fine watch. But what do you, Vishnu Maya, have to show for being a dead colonel's wife? Sore feet and a mouthful of dust."

Puffing, Gauri caught up to her sister, who strode forward, though a little slowed. "Who can tell the time in here," Vishnu Maya broke out—she poked her chest—"like we used to?" Gauri looked hard at her sister and finally guessed what she was saying. Vishnu Maya was thinking of watches, Parbati's watch. When the envy demons took hold of Vishnu Maya, there was little Gauri could do. It was no different from when your plough started sinking in the earth. You could beat the buffalo all you wanted, and the plough would dig itself forward a little. But everything was still stuck, only deeper—the plough, the buffalo and you. Anyone could see these demons of desire were a powerful force. They knew everything weak about a person before they came, then slithered slowly into the ear, coiled like a boa constrictor around the brain and squeezed. Gauri began chanting the gods' names out loud, hoping Vishnu Maya would join in. But when Vishnu Maya tried, the demons just roared louder, drowning the gods out.

That many years ago, when her husband, a Gurkha colonel in the Indian army, died, Vishnu Maya spent long months in bitter mourning. One day Raam's wife, Suniti, came to visit. "Why weep on a half-empty belly?" she said. "Why scrape a living out of these tired hills when you could get a widow's rightful pension from the army?" It was the first time Vishnu Maya knew of such a pension for widows. Of course her husband had died young. Other Gurkha pensioners in town might be retired, but they were still breathing. "A dead husband can be an asset, too," Suniti said. She explained how Vishnu Maya could have the local Brahmin write a letter, but letters more often went unanswered. The best thing to do was to go to Calcutta herself. All this time Vishnu Maya and Suniti had been drinking Suniti's homemade brew, for which she was famous in the district. Brahmins from the next village, teetotalers in the daytime, often dropped off the trail at night into Suniti's kitchen for a glass or two. She and Suniti talked and talked into late afternoon, and the more Vishnu Maya thought about it, the more she looked out over the same old hills she'd always known and saw how the jungles had disappeared and her terrace patches grown smaller and more broken up, the more Vishnu Maya thought Suniti's suggestion was a good idea. But on what was she going to make this journey? You couldn't buy bus or train tickets with a fistful of air. Suniti had thought about that, too. "I heard a woman in Pokhara gave the bank some gold jewelry as collateral," she said, "and they gave her a loan for the trip! When she came back with the pension money"—here Suniti hawked up and spat—"no problem, she paid the bank back, reclaimed her jewelry and had a bundle left over, too!"

Vishnu Maya poured them both another glass of millet whiskey. "I will do that, too," she said simply.

A week later she set off, walking three days to a town where she caught a bus. Then the hot sick-making ride to the Indian border. They crossed at night, forcing the guards out of sleep to work. One of them punched a monk and dragged away the young boy riding with him. Then there was much talk among the men, bribe talk, you could tell by the low voices and their hands. Vishnu Maya and the other passengers had to climb out of the bus and wait. The bar-bar of talk went on all night, so Vishnu Maya and the rest drew sweaters and shawls tight around them and lay down in the ditch to sleep. Next morning, when they got back on the bus, the monk was gone. Vishnu Maya was sorry; she'd been watching his glass eye.

They came to a town where Vishnu Maya was to catch a train—her first. As she stood waiting on the platform, the train farted. Vishnu Maya jumped back in fright then started laughing when the smoke rose up underneath it. Four times she got off one train and on another. Each time the train seemed to be going the wrong way, and Vishnu Maya would stare out the window, pulling at her earhole, empty now of its large gold disc in the shape of the sun. Once, as they pulled into a station, Vishnu Maya's eyes were nearly torn out of their pods by the sight of an army colonel's uniform. But the man, when she looked longer, was bald and fat, not at all like her dead husband.

The towns where the train stopped got bigger and dirtier, the food wallahs stuffing their wares through the windows shouted louder and there were more kinds of food to choose from. Squashed between a large woman who smelled of bananas and two young boys who kept shoving a fierce mongoose back in its basket, Vishnu Maya hoped they would get to Calcutta soon.

Finally they chugged into Howrah station. Vishnu Maya leaned over to take her bag from between her feet and stood up. The next thing she noticed was a strong smell of bananas and something trickling down her ear. The fat lady's face above her, breathing bananas, saying, "Wake up! Wake up! You, boy, get us some more water!" Vishnu Maya felt the hard floor of the train under her back. She thought of the filth she had seen there earlier. Her good blouse. She tried to scramble up. But hands pushed her back, voices soothed her. "Slow, slow—" they said, "what's the hurry?" Vishnu Maya had never fallen down in a dead sleep like that before, although she had heard once of a man in a distant village who fell asleep several times a day, planting seeds or eating his food, it didn't matter.

They helped her off the train, and she felt much better. The air was thick as water, but she breathed it gratefully. She was thinking about fish, about living underwater, when a young man appeared before her, made namaskaram and asked if he could help. When Vishnu Maya looked closer, she saw he was a young sahib, a sort of white man, although roasted overdone by the sun. He wore the white pajama of a peasant, but he looked well enough fed. His hair was not completely black but streaked with yellow, so it was hard to tell which color the stripes were. But he spoke in Nepali, her second language, and this was a relief amidst the foreign clatter all around them. When she told him she was looking for Indian army headquarters, he said he was just going there himself and would show her the way. Vishnu Maya was suspicious; why did this man want to help someone old enough to be his grandmother?

The young man offered to carry her bag, but Vishnu Maya gripped the strap with both hands. She pulled her shawl down over her ears in case of witches. The man said he knew a bus to catch, but Vishnu Maya said she had two legs to walk. The man jerked his head—Sure!—just like the big man in the district headquarters near Danda. His long legs settled into stride beside her.

It took them hours to get there. The hard cement under Vishnu Maya's bare feet made her ears rattle. What was the young man doing here? What did his soul desire? But he said nothing as they walked, and Vishnu Maya was too shy to ask him. The young man did not walk ahead but kept to her pace, so that after a while she began to count on the steady white strokes of his pajamas in the corners of her eyes.

At one place Vishnu Maya thought she was having a bad dream: hands—men's and women's and children's—came out of the air and grabbed at them, their sleeves and arms, her bag. But when they finally pushed through the thick forest of limbs, Vishnu Maya saw it was the young man they had been after. They smelled him coming—his business, his alms, his light skin disguised by the sun.

After that the air around them seemed brighter, tinged with mauve, her favorite color. Vishnu Maya knew she should be afraid but was not. She had heard stories of this city—her trusting countrymen robbed or beaten, hounded by witches who stole their bodies so they could wander the daytime streets, stalking nighttime prey. But the young man walked past such terrors, though they were clearly all around.

When they arrived, he leaned over, shook hands and whispered to the gateman, whom he seemed to know, and then walked back into the crowd. As Vishnu Maya watched, his shoulders dropped and his back rounded, as though he were tired or disappointed. When he turned a corner, she saw he was not the same man at all.

The guard folded something into his pocket as he led her in through the huge wooden doors of the building. In Hindi he told her where to stand. Hindi was a long-winded cousin of her second language. Vishnu Maya had to sift sounds, like market rice, through her ears just to get a few grains to chew on. She waited and waited, her legs settling like sacks of chicken feathers after the long walk. She would have squatted on the floor but was afraid when the man finally came he wouldn't see her over the high counter that came up to her chin. By the time a head appeared, the light outside the dirty windows had turned grayer. The man didn't ask her what she wanted. Instead he looked out over her head until she spoke.

"I am—" she began, but the man waved her off.

"It does not matter who you are. What is it you want?"

"My pension. I am—"

"Perhaps you have leaves stuffed in your ears," the man said. "It is nighttime now, as you may have noticed." He motioned with his chin to the dusty window. "The working day is over. You will have to come back tomorrow, when we are open."

"But the guard—"

"The guard is as stupid as you," said the man. "Come when we are open only." He turned and went back through a door. As it closed Vishnu Maya heard a guffaw and the unmistakable clap of playing cards on wood.

That evening, faint with hunger, Vishnu Maya found a temple where they would feed her for a rupee and let her sleep on the floor. As darkness fell, more and more people came out of the air, like ghosts. She found herself near the end of the line for food, and then when she had gobbled down the small portion of gray daal and tasteless rice, she had to wake some people up and ask them to make room on the floor.

The next morning, at first light, Vishnu Maya walked back to the army headquarters. This time the guard was asleep behind the gate, which was padlocked. Vishnu Maya squatted down on the sidewalk and watched the early morning rise. First a few street dwellers lit their fires for morning tea. One young girl brought her a cup, and Vishnu Maya drank it gratefully. The girl's mother, whose cup it was, nodded over to Vishnu Maya and smiled. After a time the street dwellers took their shawls and cups and moved off, and rickshaws and taxis broke the peaceful line of her sight. *rrrrrRRRR! rrrrrrRRRRR!* The engines made Vishnu Maya's head ache, and the clacking cartwheels made her dizzy. The sun, what was left of it, was high up in the sky when the guard finally opened the gate. Some noisy jeeps raced through importantly, spraying her with a fine layer of dust.

Vishnu Maya hurried in the gate and up through the wooden doors. But inside, the benches were already taken up with bored-looking men, every one of them expecting to be served before the others. So Vishnu Maya stood near the door, which by now had gained a doorman. When someone else came, the doorman, who had a monstrous head, jabbed a stubby finger in the air, pointing first at Vishnu Maya, then at a spot on the floor further from the lineup of men on the benches. Vishnu Maya looked straight into his eyes, defying his orders, but the doorman grunted and jabbed his finger more frighteningly, and Vishnu Maya didn't want to make trouble. She moved a few inches, not quite as far as the man was pointing. Two, three more people came, four, five, and each time the doorman's menacing finger pointed Vishnu Maya further back in line. Vishnu Maya was just about to shove forward around the man in brown khaki in front of her, when a name was called and the brown khaki walked forward. Vishnu Maya quickly darted up in his place to watch the proceedings.

Behind the tall counter, a head appeared, the same one as yesterday. After a long conversation, the head directed the khaki man across the room where a uniformed clerk sat behind a desk piled high with paper. His hands were folded on one bare spot before him. The two talked in low voices for a moment, and then the clerk pointed back to the head. The khaki man walked back to the high counter, where the head motioned him back to this seat.

By the time the next man was called, Vishnu Maya lost interest. She was watching the clerk nearest to her; he looked small in that huge room. He picked up a file from the pile on the left corner of his desk and placed it in front of him. Then he opened it slowly, as though underwater. He gazed at the file for a long time. Then he closed it again and laid it carefully in the empty right-hand corner of his desk and folded his hands on the empty space the file had left.

There was a sudden flurry, and a boy appeared from the door where Vishnu Maya had heard the cards slap yesterday. In his hand a little metal rack held four glasses of steaming tea. The boy took these around to four of the clerks, then went back through the office door. He repeated this several times until all the clerks were served, at which time they closed whatever was open before them, put down their pens, motioned the petitioners back to their seats and sat back to enjoy the tea. Vishnu Maya was bewildered. She had never been in such a busy office before; once or twice she had looked in at the district headquarters near her village, but there were only two men there and even then only part of the year.

The sun began to fade, and Vishnu Maya could see they wouldn't get to her before closing. She looked over at the clerk; he coddled a finger's width of tea like a cracked egg. Vishnu Maya wadded up some phlegm with her tongue and blew it out the large gap between her front teeth, which she'd found useful many times for this purpose. *Zzzzzzssst!* The gob of spit landed a hand's length from his shoe, but the clerk paid no attention. He was staring into his tea glass, one hand digging absently around in his ear. *Zzzzzzzsssst!* Vishnu Maya sent another spit wad flying in his direction, this time landing only a hair's width from the toe of his shoe. The clerk looked up; the sound alerted him rather than the pinkish spittle, which he still had not noticed. Vishnu Maya started to talk, explaining the mix-up with her pension, but the clerk cupped his ear and pointed to his mouth, shook his head and smiled. Vishnu Maya couldn't make out what he meant; if he was deaf, why had he looked up? For the first time since the Brahmin read her the letter of her husband's death, Vishnu Maya felt her throat grow thick with tears. She felt for the prayer beads hidden in her skirt, held them for a moment, feeling their warmth in her palm. When the choking feeling subsided a little, she mumbled some of the more powerful gods' names to herself. They comforted her. Today was inauspicious, they assured her, for getting things done. Still talking with the gods, Vishnu Maya turned and walked out the door, which creaked louder each time someone came or went. She made her way back to the temple to wait for dawn.

Next morning Vishnu Maya took her time getting to the army building. Now the guard pretended not to understand her. "You won't get anywhere speaking with that gravel in your mouth," he said, "and besides, you stupid woman, we're closed today. I suppose, up in those hills, you haven't heard of Saturday! Ha! Ha!" He held his stomach. "Now go back up to that thin air you suck, and don't bother these busy men anymore with your delusions."

Vishnu Maya's eyes narrowed into slits. "I saw you put that sahib's money in your pocket," she said. "I see now how justice works in this cesspool." She thrust her hand up, worked her fingers under his nose. "Baksheesh, baksheesh! That's how your busy men give out their justice! The poor wife of a colonel did not come down to hell to make a deal!" She spat on the guard's shoe and stalked off before he could hit her. The guard staggered a little when his hand slapped air.

On the way back to Nepal, Vishnu Maya stopped at an important temple. Three sacred rivers met there, one coming from the north, another from the south and the third flowing up from the center of the earth. The guru at the temple told Vishnu Maya about the third river; otherwise she might not have noticed. Guru taught her to meditate, too. He told her a mantra chant: *Sri Ram, Je Ram, Je Je Ram, Om.* Vishnu Maya sat in a corner somewhere or down on the steps beside the river and repeated it over and over, but she could never say the words as fast as Guru could. This chanting wasn't as easy as he made it seem; she couldn't let her mind go to sleep or amble around where it wanted. It was more like jumping over evenly spaced stones: she might bounce up in a kind of rhythm, but she couldn't fly off.

One morning, after a few weeks of temple life, Vishnu Maya woke up earlier than usual; as soon as she walked out of the sleep house, she saw why. The river was calling her to bathe, now, before the others arose. So Vishnu Maya walked straight in, her knees pressing the slow current. Then collapsed, as though a great weight had been lifted from her back. When her head resurfaced, Vishnu Maya was smiling, her mouth a black hole in the darkness. She felt the cool water roll off her as she rose; it swirled and cascaded from her nostrils, mouth, forehead, ears, from her shoulders and along her fingers. Her long braid streamed and streamed down her back. Now Vishnu Maya understood the language of the river, which only reminded her of the duty she'd been shirking. She unplaited her old hair and let it hang loose in the widow's way. She scrubbed her arms vigorously, her legs, her face and neck, and under her clothes, as much of her body as she was able. Thus cleansed of her husband's death pollution, Vishnu Maya felt with her left hand along her right arm. Her fingertips gathered the glass wedding bangles down from her elbow to her wrist. Then she squeezed her right palm together the way it had been squeezed those years ago. One or two or three of these bangles were original, but Vishnu Maya had forgotten which ones. The old woman pushed the bangles along her cramped wet hand. One at the end she couldn't catch. It fell off in the black water. The rest she took good hold of and heaved toward the stone ghat on the bank. They splintered like musical notes in the damp air.

The current prodding her downstream, Vishnu Maya waded slowly back toward the bank. There was no more reason for her to stay here. She gathered up the few things in her little cell, placed the cloth strap of her bag over her forehead in the old way of hill people. Something passed over her, both happy and sad, like a beautiful bird with its shadow. Was she going to cry or laugh? Vishnu Maya didn't know. She did know this long train journey, the good people and not-so-good, the fine holy men in their temple were like a person's lost soul flying around the cremation ground at night. The lamas could chase the glittering butterfly around all night, but whether or not they caught it in their urn, at daybreak they had to come home. It seemed to Vishnu Maya that morning had arrived. Quietly, so as not to disturb anyone, Vishnu Maya walked down the temple steps and along to the train station and bought her first ticket toward home.

When she got there, nothing had changed. Except her gold would no longer adorn wrists and ears and ankles but instead would line the steel vault at the bank.

Now Surya was beginning to descend in his chariot, always Vishnu Maya's favorite time of day. In the gap between the valley walls ahead, a golden carpet spread before them. There, where the ground was so briefly molten, the sisters came to another village with very narrow stone streets and houses. Outside the village, the land played a joke—lemon, banana, orange and apple trees burst up from the well-irrigated earth. The sisters agreed it was like heaven. There they were told about sacred fossils higher up—black ancient rocks with creatures locked inside. From here they would reach their destination in a day. When they got there, the sacred rocks were obvious, not just from the black color but also from the heat pouring backward out of them into the air. It was easy to see the spiritual power of stones like these. The two sisters sat among them a long time, running their fingers over the tiny spines and tails and what could have been fins, squeezing the jagged corners until they bit into the flesh of their hands. Walking again, they tried not to step on the fossils, but it wasn't easy—the creatures swam, crept, slept all around them. Near the end of the fossil field, something winked in the bottom of Vishnu Maya's eye. Letting Gauri go by, she stooped down for a closer look. There, locked in black, a tiny white fan, a shell such as her daughter's father had brought home once, years ago, from an Indian beach. Vishnu Maya ran her fingers over the stone, closed her eyes. By touching only, she would never have known the shell was there. She brought the stone to her nose and sniffed, stuck out her tongue and licked. Nothing. Nothing there. But for the proof of eyes. Sliding the shell stone into her waistband, Vishnu Maya stood up. In no time at all, she saw the red, green and blue flowers of Gauri's skirt winding up the gray rocks ahead.

By now the landscape was nothing but rocks, not a patch of grass to piss in anywhere. Vishnu Maya had heard about the awful barrenness; now they were inside it. At first she thought, *How can people live here?* But they drove their loaded yaks right by her, pulled small dirty potatoes out of the earth despite her doubts. She saw there was soil after all and stone-fenced fields all around her, drier and browner than she was used to, swaying with grain.

They stopped for a rest on the top of the last ridge. Some local people joined them; they had come up the other side. Four women and a man, long braids wrapping their heads, silver and turquoise and coral swinging from their ears and necks, cheekbones, quick peaks under smooth brown skin. Strange language slicing from their tongues. As they chattered to each other, tossing a word now and then to the sisters, Vishnu Maya kept coming back to the man's eyes. They puffed up like chappatis on a fire. The whites, most of the eyes themselves, were lost in curves and folds. Eyes like these she had never seen before—protected, hidden, with a traveling spark like a flaw spinning in glass. Vishnu Maya gazed back down the long valley she had come from. The river they had followed gleamed like golden hair in the sun. Vishnu Maya tried to imagine flying up from this mountainside to the top of Mount Dhauligiri or higher. Sooner or later she knew she would see other strands, other rivers join with this one, flow together, meet thicker and thicker hairs until they buried themselves in Mother Ganges' deep tresses. Vishnu Maya looked back into the eyes of the braided man. They were not strange at all but familiar. Not distinct but common, and she had only been fooled by their separate faces: her father, her daughter's father, her son-in-law, the guard at the army headquarters in Calcutta, the head behind the tall counter. Vishnu Maya tried to picture the young sahib, the burnt-skin man who appeared years ago, bribed the gateman, then vanished in a crowd. She saw the details of his sandaled foot, long toes squared as though by a wood-carver's chisel. Then the brown ankle and calf stuffing the lower pajama leg. Higher up, the half-heard whisper of thigh where it brushed flaring cotton. She saw the long tunic, hanging baglike over his belly's absence, and his shoulders, not wide, their smooth curving into throat and cheek, like the stem of a blowing tree. But in the frame of his face, she saw only a fallow field, the eyes a soft brown center, shadow, then nothing at all.

Where had the stranger come from those years ago? Why had he guided her through Calcutta's terrors? It seemed to Vishnu Maya this appearance must have been an auspicious sign. Then why did she fail so miserably at army headquarters? Why, when she remembers India, does her head rattle and her stomach fall down like she was on a festival swing? Why does she recall suffering, feel the bite of humiliation all over again? Maybe the charred sahib had been an unlucky sign. But why would Bhagwan or another god want to confuse her? Why turn a young man's kindness into loss and shame? Even if the gods had left her and some devil seen his chance to play, why would he choose some poor hill woman out of all those throngs, a woman lost in a strange country, bringing nothing with her, no wealth of any kind, but only a fair claim? No matter which thought-strand she chased, the answer disappeared before Vishnu Maya could catch it, just like the young man's face. The blood in her feet started boiling up her legs. Vishnu Maya could not sit any longer. Crossing her feet under her, she sprang up. Her bag flew from one hand behind her until, already many paces down the trail, she fixed it back on her head. Gauri, who by now had scrambled to her feet, hurried behind her sister down the last stretch toward Muktinath.

The wind nipped at their cheeks, licked and howled around their faces. The two old women dug into their bags for more cotton layers. Their hands retreated in the sleeves of their sweaters. The sun paled, got tired, then left them. Rising before them on the horizon, four gray ghosts. Vishnu Maya touched Gauri's arm. Gauri had seen them, too. The sisters stopped and stood for a long time, afraid to go on. Vishnu Maya thought of the time she had malaria or something like it; her visions were good then, even in the middle of her fevers. She saw green healthy fields and tall evenly spaced trees right from the door of her house. Was this bad vision a trick of the holy shrine? In Kathmandu, terrifying carved images drove evil spirits away from the sacred temples. The sisters stood holding each other, waiting to see if the ghosts would move. When they did not, Vishnu Maya and Gauri decided they should either risk going on or sleep out in the cold. As they approached, the haze in their eyes cleared; they remembered the old tales. Here, then, were the four stone villages of Muktinath. And there, off to one side, just as the stories had told, rose the holy temple and shrines where, it was said, the Buddha himself danced forever.

In the dying light, the two sisters ran under each of the one hundred and three cold water spouts. Then they ran back through again. And again. It turned into a game; neither would give up before the other. Then Gauri, eyes clenched against the freezing water, ran—*Kar-PLUK!*—straight into her sister. But Vishnu Maya was like a stone, immovable. At the mouth of one spout, carved in the shape of a cow's head, with water pouring down the tongue, Maya stood staring. Gauri had heard tell of how, long ago, Krishna opened a cow's mouth for his mother and told her to look in. There she saw the universe. Gauri poked like a hen around Vishnu Maya's head, trying to get a view. But she could not see what Vishnu Maya saw:

The braid-headed man and the women, descending that big hill under a high sun, chattering and laughing about the two old lowland women on their way to Muktinath. Vishnu Maya saw the villages, bridges, rocky streams and farmsteads she and Gauri had passed. Black-skinned porters under dirty white sacks of salt and rice. The father toting his sick daughter in a basket on his back. The bhatti where they spent yesterday night: the woman there swept the floor after they left. Downstream a little, before they woke up, a man held a finger line, fishing. In the next village down, the day before yesterday, a class of schoolboys moved benches out into the sun. The boy who sold them bananas the day before that counted the rupees two old women had paid him, then walked over to his friend for a game of cards. These days boys bought cigarettes with their parents' money, then made playing cards out of the packages. Then they played for more money—what could anyone do! Some army patrols played football at half-moon—a week ago. The black and white ball flickered on the night. Behind the game, trees brooded, black sentries, the sky joined its black hand to the ground. Inside the forest, no one could tell up from down. The eye darted this way and that, searching for a streak of light. Then Vishnu Maya spied a pinpoint of orange, like the end of a cigarette. And then, like a dead person's soul watching relatives grieve over the body, she saw her village, her friends and neighbors and family—her daughter and grandchildren! It was the night, months ago, of the annual scabies exorcism. They threw a bucket of coals—*phiishhh!*—hot stars, into the dark.

Then Vishnu Maya gasped, for she saw herself, but a young self, not long after she was married. She was living in her parents' house still. The night for sarad, the meal they cooked once a year for the deceased relatives who came after dark to eat. She was up already, about to start preparing the meal, when her friends came by. "You can do that after you play with us awhile," they said. And Vishnu Maya had gone with them to the rodi house and laughed and played until dawn. When she came home and fell asleep, all the dead ancestors were waiting there to scold her.

But even their angry voices soon became like the drone of bees under a new brassy sound. The noise Vishnu Maya dreaded, moving closer, closer. She was fifteen years old, hiding in their cornfield, shaking with fear. Her palms were soaked with sweat, and the soil stuck darkly in the lines, as though to highlight the fate written there. The wedding band moved closer, her future husband would be with them, all of them coming to fetch her. She heard them stop at her house; through the leaves she could just make out the boy all in white. After some time she heard sharp voices, shouts, her name. Some men trampled the bushes near her house, looking; others were dispatched through the village to enquire of the neighbors. Vishnu Maya grew weary, squatting; she hadn't slept all night, planning her early escape. She sat and then lay down, hugging the comforting bases of cornstalks, and drifted into sleep. When the sun was high over the west ridge, she woke to the hum of voices at the door to her father's house. She saw her father (her mother was already dead then) coax Gauri, who was only eight or nine, from inside to stand before the men. It was bad luck for a groom's party to return to his village without a bride. More talk, more men were deployed. Just before nightfall, someone caught sight of Vishnu Maya's gold bracelet in the last blaze of the setting sun. He pulled her by the ear back to the house, where, seated beside her new husband on her father's porch, a paste of colored rice pressed on her forehead in blessing, Vishnu Maya cried and cried.

Night fell and out of the darkness flew high voices, singing. Vishnu Maya recognized the refrain and the sweet familiar voices of her youth. It was that night in the year when all the unmarried girls and boys line up on either side of the village to play at question-and-answer songs until sunrise. "If you are so beautiful and clever, then why do you spend your days digging in the earth and carrying dung?" came a boy's voice. Then there was a chorus of voices, singing the refrain. Out of the night from the other direction, a girl sang in rhyme, "With village boys all as ugly and lazy as you to choose from, I'd rather carry dung at my parents' home than suffer the burden of your base desires." Vishnu Maya's face grew hot; her shoulders flinched. That was her voice. But she barely had time to take this in when the chorus rang again. Then the boy's voice, clear and serious—her husband, Ram Raj. "I see you are waiting for a wealthy army man to take you around the world, but where is he? When you are an old woman, will you pull him from your goiter?" Vishnu Maya's mouth felt tight. Her arms grew hot. When a girl stopped responding to the boy's parries, she was obliged to marry him. The long contest went on all night, while underneath ran a continuous high-spirited hum—the hasty, coaching whispers of the other girls and boys. Toward dawn, weak with laughter and mental exhaustion, chilled by dew, Vishnu Maya began to shiver. Something tugged her arm. "Come away," said Gauri, "it's too cold staying here. Your skin feels like chicken flesh."

While they changed into dry clothes behind a chorten, Vishnu Maya told Gauri all the things she had seen in the cow's mouth. "It was the past I was seeing," she said, "but it felt like the future."

"You were looking in no longer than it takes the tongue of a Brahmin to scrape the bottom of a raksi glass," Gauri said. "How could you see all that?"

They went into the holiest part, then, where the caretaker showed them a great stone Buddha. While the sisters made offerings of incense, grain and rupees, all the stored-up eager prayers fell over their tongues trying to get out. Then the caretaker beckoned them over to a dark corner of the room, pulling aside as he did so a heavy drape, the same maroon color as his robe. There, on the *shusshh* of a sacred spring, danced a many-colored flame.

On the way back home to Danda, Vishnu Maya said to her sister, "Our fields and animals are crying for their old mothers."

A while later Gauri said, "Is the flame still dancing in your eyes? Maya closed her eyes to see. Behind the lids . . . yes, a quick flicker, dancing light. Purple and blue and red and green and white. "Older sister?" Gauri said.

But Vishnu Maya still did not open her eyes. For there, rising around the flame on either side, like a great double-necked beast out of the water, were the blue legs of the Sleeping Vishnu, just as they'd appeared at Budhanilkantha so long ago—bent up slightly, crossed at the ankles, spreading the smooth stone thighs. Vishnu Maya opened her eyes. "Yes," she replied, "it is there."

She and Gauri collected some stones and rocks and then built a cairn together, a reminder to the gods of their pilgrimage. After piling the rocks in a cone, the sisters felt light as birds. They hooked their hands on their head sacks and skipped a little down the trail like girls, giggling, excited. Vishnu Maya felt something burning in the pit of her stomach, but it was not like the burning from eating food a witch had served you. Nor was it like the hot poker of shame. This fire warmed her up to dancing heat.

When they came again to the hot pool of water, Vishnu Maya plucked the bottle from her sack. She poured the remaining fire down her throat and plunged into the water with the bottle, filling it as she went. Her sister, guessing at Vishnu Maya's plan, said, "This rotten-egg water will be cold by the time we get home."

"But will the spices run out?" Vishnu Maya said. "If I sprinkle this water on my garden, will more hot water not grow up?"

One slanting afternoon, they came to a familiar tree, then a hill and a view they knew well. As they descended into Danda, Gauri said, "In that cow's mouth, did you see your family?"

"Yes," said Vishnu Maya.

"All of them or just some?"

"All of them," said Vishnu Maya, "although some people were probably inside their houses cooking." Gauri didn't speak. "There were so many people in that cow's mouth," Vishnu Maya said, "no one in the world was somewhere else."

"Oh, little sister, do you remember when we were girls, those pensioners brought that black and white ball for football to the village? They kicked it over the field, and it bounced an hour's walk into that old man's cornfield."

"Yes, I remember," laughed Gauri. "He took it to a Brahmin in the next village to ask what sign the gods had sent him for his crop yield!"

At last they saw their villages, like soft green moss under cracked callouses. Vishnu Maya pointed to her own rice and cornfields. "They grow well considering I wasn't here to watch those lazy sharecroppers," she said. Then wished she hadn't spoken. Words, she saw now, could sometimes cloud the soul. Leaving Gauri at her doorstep, Vishnu Maya continued down the path to her village. She saw the roof of her little house, thatched with her own hands in the old way young people had now forgotten. Saw her dear old buffalo waiting in her stall to be milked. It was good, good to be home. How long she had waited to lie down on her own mat!

Vishnu Maya woke early. She squatted by the copper water urn, drew the tumpline down over her forehead. Stood up and padded through the darkness to the far spring—the nearby one her neighbors used was muddy this time of year. The cat following her, as always, about halfway. She returned, hands hooked on the rope at her temples, the day's water jogging at her back. Dipping some water out of the jug into a small bowl, Vishnu Maya splashed her face, while chanting the names of the gods, as she did every morning and evening: YE ISWAR VISHNU BHAGWAN VISHNU JAGGANATH PASHUPATINATH SWYAMBUNATH MUKTINATH. . . .

Then she approached the water buffalo, who rubbed her head against the rough boards of her stall, making her neck chain rumble. Vishnu Maya placed the milk pail under the udders and began to pull. A little came, not much; the buffalo was getting old. In the house she lit the fire and brewed tea, poured a little of the creamy milk in with two spoonfuls of sugar and drank quickly. She washed the cup out and replaced it on its shelf. She swept the floor, flinging bits of mud and grass expertly over the step into the darkness. Yesterday she had freshly plastered the floor and porch steps with a mixture of red clay and buffalo dung. Cow dung would have been better—more powerful spiritually—but her cousin's cow had been out grazing somewhere. Vishnu Maya looked around, making sure everything was in order for her daughter's family to look after.

She took up the small bag she had packed last night with a change of clothes, a sweater and a full bottle of Kukri rum. Something fell out of her waist as she put out the lantern, a small stone. Vishnu Maya grumbled, picked it up and flung it out the door, then walked down the step and up the path toward her sister's house in Danda. The chill earth under her bare feet reminded her of something, a dream. But Vishnu Maya knew better than to chase it—if it wanted to visit again, this dream, it would. At the moment, she was eager to get to Gauri's to begin their pilgrimage together, as arranged.

HEAVEN, THE RAIN GOD, THIS WORLD, WOMAN

Out of the hot mouth of India we gallop. Iron horse, nightmare, fleeing what we are: neither coarse nor fine, shadow nor darkness; neither short nor long, substance nor attribute. If we speak, the noise is fire, our breath, the wind feeding fire. In our sides wink the worlds' suns, our ears hoot direction. Awake, in sleeping arms, I rock. In the loneliness of mother sleeping, nothing satisfies thought. Nothing but the moon-bright shadow of a train, my coursing future. And I, no bigger than a mote in the sun, one tiny carriage eye.

When I am four, squatting on strange sand. In a country called Norway that sometimes smells like Canada, when the wind blows toward you through the pines. When the slush melts. It is ocean now, a beach, and in the beach, tiny, tiny specks of sand. Something. Scut-scuttle. Crab, says my father, land crab. Crab-wabby! I shout, for fear of dart, of leg manyness (how many?) Crab-wabby! fa/mother roar, their mouths swallowing fear. Here, crab, here! Sand creeping many scuttleness. *Please run,* I pray to the crab. *Please run away.*

It is called a holiday. I sleep in the car with my sisters. I get the front seat because I'm only six and smallest. They fold down behind. Fa/mother sleep in the tent, which father ties to the car bumper with a rope. So we don't blow away, he says, and winks, your mother and I. That night in the crying wind I dream a car, our yellow Taunus, with a blue and orange canvas tent, like a satellite—a word I have just learned. The Taunus and tent fly together across the moon. Underneath, brown wooden buildings with curved roofs—peaks layered like cakes. I know what these are called from my mother—stave churches.

We are on our way north, up the thin neck of Norway to the Arctic Circle. We play games. How wide is the skinniest part of the neck? we ask my father who has given us the map. Maybe five, ten miles. Which? Maybe ten. We visit a cave, black and green and gray inside, dripping. We look at a rock with a piece of metal on it, shiny black with sad numbers. There is a picture of a man's head on the metal, but his name is written too high for me to see. Edvard Grieg, my sister reads, and mother says, that's right. Is the dead man in the rock? What, dear? says my mother. Is the dead man in the rock? I say. He's in a vault, she says, where you can't see. What's a vault? It's like a big box, says my mother, you lock up with a key. Later we eat corned beef sandwiches in the car beside the road, when my mother gets out in a hurry. Where's she going? To the backhouse, says my father, and laughs. I don't see any houses, though, just trees. Dad, do dead people go to heaven? Usually . . . he says . . . then: As far as I know. When they go there, do they have to take a key? Well, well, my father laughs again, I suppose they would now, wouldn't they? How else would they open up those goddamn pearly gates? he says.

We are driving again. I look at the map my sisters hold between them in the backseat, then roll over on my back. I like it here, jammed up high against the cool of the rear window, looking at the sky. I'm the only one who fits. What's the blue? What blue? says my father. On the map. Water, the ocean, says my father. Why? Why what? Why is it blue? You've seen the ocean. It was green with black strings in it, they don't show the black strings. From far away, says my father, you can't see the seaweed, and the water looks blue. Why? Why what? Why faraway? Then I am flying out of my cool glass bed, over my sisters' heads, toward mother and father, the rushing rocks and trees called scenery. But now the scenery has stopped. WHOOPS! says my father, and my mother says, OHMYGODINHEAVEN! And I am looking at my sister's feet, my face jammed downward between her legs and the back of mother's seat. Are you all all right—where's your sister? says my father. Down here, says my sister, tweaking my nose with her foot. Get her up, for heaven's sake. Pulling one arm, twisting my head. Bloody cow, says my father and starts the engine, which stalled when he stepped on the brake. Ahhhh! . . . says my mother, it's just a little calf—look kids! I half-sit, half-lie across my sisters' laps. The three of us press our noses to the glass. A spindly calf totters after its mother through the ditch. I want to roll down the window and talk to it, tell it everything's okay. But we are already too far down the road for that. My arms and legs are hot and sweaty against my sisters'; they're squirming under me, pushing me away. Now I remember what I was going to say. If the blue is ocean, and we don't stop soon . . . but there is still the gray ribbon of road in front of us, more rocks and stubby trees. We are not at the edge yet.

We see Lapps, their skin the color of toast. They wear hats with flapping ears, soft furry coats and boots. My father says they herd reindeer, and we see those, too, their coats stripping off like banana peels. Later, in the lightness of night, I can't sleep. Just close your eyes, says my mother, and rest.

Rest is nearly as good. I pull the sleeping bag over my head in my bed on the front seat. Inside, I dream furry-faced people pulling the skin off reindeer with their teeth. The reindeer groan, sigh with relief. This skin is too hot, they nod, red hats flopping against their cheeks.

One day, in the pouring rain, we pull off to read a sign. WELCOME TO THE LAND OF THE MIDNIGHT SUN, my father reads aloud. He puts out his hands, palms up, winks at me. In the car my middle sister beckons to me with her finger. This means she is going to tell me a secret. That or spit in my ear. I take a chance on the secret. She cups her hands around my ear. Just then there is a crack of thunder, a bolt of lightning rips open the sky. I want to dive under the seat, but my sister doesn't flinch, so neither do I. Hear that? she hisses, meaning the thunder. I nod, unable to speak, as though she's got hold of my tongue, not my ear. When thunder and lightning are close together like that, she whispers, it means it's near. My sister knows about a lot of things that I don't; there is no reason to disbelieve her. I start to pull away; her warm wet breath is tickling my ear. But she won't let go. You know what thunder is? she breathes. I shake again. It's Thor roaring. He's angry, it means. Now I do push her away. I will ignore her. I look away, but there is nothing to see. Rain-sheeted window. I slide my eyes over, watch my sister instead. She is staring at the window the way grown-ups do, looking past the pane itself into space. What can she see there, I wonder, that I can't? Her eye, for all its distance, falls short of the glass, too. I poke her shoulder, cup my mouth to her ear. Who's Thor? I whisper loudly. She doesn't answer me in speech but takes a pencil out of the holder my father has fixed for our things behind his seat. In a small blank space on the map, she prints something so small I can't see. That is, until she holds it up against my nose, forcing me to read: THOR IS A GIANT MAGIC MAN WHO LIVES BEHIND THE

CLOUDS, WHERE YOU CAN'T SEE. IF HE IS ANGRY WITH SOMEONE, HE STRIKES THEM WITH HIS MAGIC HAMMER. And they . . .

The print gets smaller and smaller, so the last few words take some time to read.

. . . sizzle into . . .

Now my other sister wants to see. She starts pulling it away as I read.

. . . nothing on . . .

They each jab a finger in my ribs.

. . . the spot.

It's been a trick. When the tickling is over, with my father's stern voice riding over top, I feel like throwing up. It's bad enough tossing back and forth on this road, without tickling sisters. And now Thor, the angry magic man pitching lightning down around us, trying to melt us to a stop.

My ninth birthday is in a province called PEI. We drive for two days from Ontario to get there and stay in my cousins' cottage on a red beach. Their last name is the same as my mother's old one. My father calls this the back side of the Island and tells me to smile at my cousins when I don't. What I am waiting for is the beach.

The bedroom is cold, a big closet with material across for a door. There is just enough room inside for some bunks and a chair, a tiny window that looks back out on the cars. I peel off my car-sweaty clothes and shiver into my new bathing suit, bought on the way in Montreal. It is a black and gold tiger-striped two-piece with black fishnet in the middle. My mother wanted to get me a blue one-piece with a little skirt. But I put this one on the counter first, and the beautiful black-haired lady, who was speaking French at the same time on the phone, rang it in like nothing and handed me the bag. The lady was still on the phone as my mother sorted the coins and paper change into her purse. She gave us this one, Mom, I said, and opened the bag for her to see. My mother hardly even looked. Oh, that's all right, she said in a tired way to the back of the lady's head, already turned to the phone.

We dig clams. The gold hairs on my uncle's chest lead us into the falling sun. My cousins make fun of my black fishnet. Dad, maybe we should look for sharks instead, they say, pointing. My uncle smiles, says nothing to discourage them, and I am disappointed. I look down past my itchy midriff, see the splashes of red mud across my thighs. I look over at my boy cousin, Chad, in ripped jean shorts and no shirt, my girl cousin, Lisa, in a baggy gray swimsuit that looks as though it used to be blue. They are both covered in mud, head to toe; it is in their hair, along the insides of their arms. My own arms seem pale and sickly beside theirs, but when I touch one to Lisa's and compare, it is almost the same color brown.

First you have to find a clam. Lisa shows me the little holes in the sand they breathe through. When you have picked out a good hole, you have to dig like hell, says my uncle. There, he says. Try that one. He thrusts the shovel in my hands and shows me how to hold it. But I am much too slow, and the clam disappears before I can even see it.

One day I come home from school, and there are two strangers on the doorstep in suits talking to my mother, who is mostly hidden behind the screen. It is odd for anyone to be supplicant on a doorstep in Mountain River. It's a small town, mostly we would know or recognize anyone who came. The strangers, whose hair is short, aggressively out of style, look as if they're trying to sell my mother something, but their hands are strangely empty, and there is no car to be seen. I catch my mother's words as I turn up the drive. No, in this house we pretty much believe in evolution. Thanks just the same. This quick thinking of my mother seems to have worked. The strangers turn away from the door. And now I see they are not entirely empty-handed—one holds a black leather-bound Bible in his hand. They smile as we pass in the driveway, but this does not make me feel better, as adult smiling normally would. Instead our driveway suddenly looks gritty, the view in our open garage untidy, careless. When I open the screen door, my mother has her back to me. Through the hall, in the kitchen, I see her standing in front of the sink, plunging her rubber-gloved hands in soapy water, clattering dishes and pots and cutlery into the rack as though she were in a hurry.

I snap on the TV to my favorite show, *The Forest Rangers*. Chubb and Kathy and Indian Joe are already embroiled in another adventure. Usually I can pick up what's going on. But today I'm restless, I keep staring out the window. I know why we believe in evolution. It's because we're scientific, like most other families in town. I watch the short-haired men with the Bible getting turned away, door after door. I feel sad for them, sort of, but not the way I feel sad when a baby bear gets caught in the man-trap Indian Joe helps Chubb and Kathy make. They're trying to catch some poachers in the area, not bears—that's what they're trying to save. No, I feel sad the way I do when people pass by crippled Mr. MacNulty's table at the Christmas bazaar, which seems, year after year, to offer the wrong thing.

Mountain River, as everyone in the region knows, is full of scientists and their families; the men have PhDs. Creation, to us, is matter exploding—a big bang. They pick it up as background noise on special instruments at the research labs where our fathers work. I've heard it myself, at open house last year. These strange shorn men—so earnestly outdated—did they not know what they were getting into? What must it be like to stand on our hot doorsteps in itchy suits, holding out hope we don't want, a heaven we can't see?

I am thirteen years old when my childhood indifference to crows is wiped out completely and forever. The film club shows Alfred Hitchcock's *The Birds* after school. When the lights come back on and the venetian blinds are turned, it is dark outside.

The school door snaps, metallic, behind me, locks me in the late November air. I have never been afraid of the dark, but now I watch the trees, duck at a shadow. Black wings beat at my chest, my stomach, around my head. When I turn into our driveway, my foot hits something soft, solid. Hey! don't bust your old man's ribs! I look down. My father is lying on his back on the pavement, his binoculars surprised away from his eyes.

What're you doing, Dad? Contemplating the heavens, is that all right? His voice isn't jokey anymore but rides that edge I've learned to skirt. I say nothing, look up at the sky. Wanna look? He flings the hand holding the binoculars toward me. They are heavy unexpected weight, but I manage to hold on. I lift, turn skyward, lower them onto my eyes. You won't see anything that way, my father says. You can't hold them still. I can and do hold them still—my steady hand has always been a secret source of pride. But I get down beside him on the drive to save us both my contradiction. Do you know what you're looking for? he says, as if I should. I want to giggle, somehow, but this, in our unspoken universe, is not allowed. The Milky Way? I suggest hopefully, racking my brains for his enthusiasms of the past. Craters in the moon? Oh, he mumbles, as though this is not the first time he's forgotten something. He points off in the dark. You see my hand? I pull my head up to look, and the muscles in my stomach begin to shake. I can see a dark arm floating in dark, but I can't see where he is pointing, exactly. His black-gloved hand is gone, severed, it seems, at the fine pale line of wrist between glove and sleeve. You see the North Star? he says. Uhhhh . . . I scan the sky frantically, feeling his impatience. There, in the north, as you might expect, he says. His hands come up behind me, around my head. He knocks my temple, accidentally—WHOOP!—then pushes the binoculars around in the proper direction. I still don't see much. He's knocked the eye pieces further apart, blurring my view. I close one eye, try to focus on the sky, but if the North Star is there, there's nothing to distinguish it from the rest. My father lets go of the binoculars before I am ready. They drop painfully against the socket bones of my eyes. Doesn't matter, he says, disgusted, I think. He blows in his gloves, folds his arms across his chest—BRRRR! What, if anything, *do* you see, for God's sake? Nothing, until I take the glasses away from my eyes. Just then something pulses, a kind of glow. Here, says my father and yanks the binoculars away. Now I do see something—it is getting brighter; pale streaks, green flames leap across the sky. You won't see *that* in a city, says my father. What? Dear God, child, the Northern Lights! says my father, and tightens the black tubes against the sockets of his eyes. Don't they teach you anything in school?

My father and I lie side by side on the driveway. My mother cooks dinner against the kitchen window, in the corner of my eye. The cold stiffens under my thin coat, but I do not move. Instead I imagine flying into the space between the stars. It is hard to keep up there, though, with my back arching off the freezing ground. Again and again I fling myself up in the sky, am pulled back down.

That spring my father goes to India on business, brings back silk for my mother and sisters, an elaborate Indian doll for me. The doll is for my collection of foreign dolls, a round, brown, classical dancer clad in red and gold. One of her legs is planted solidly, the bent knee turned out over her bare foot, the other pulled straight—you can feel the muscle tension—just the heel touching an imaginary floor and the foot flexed back toward her shin. Her arms dance away from her body in sharp angles; one hand is flexed backward at the wrist, the fingers pointed to the ground, while the other, also flexed, is held back behind her head, its palm open to the sky. Her pupils do not focus forward but stretch tight against the corners of her eyes. I rearrange the other dolls on my shelf—Annalisa, Edvard, Eva, Colleen, Marie, Renato—as her audience and do not give her a name.

My father also brings back slides to show us what India looks like, and another place, further north, called Nepal, where they took a red-eye tour. I'm not sure what my father means by this. I can't imagine my father's eyes with red dots painted in the inner corners, like my doll. Be grateful for winter, he says, when I say India looks nice and warm. In India you'd burn to a frazzle in no time at all. My mother, my sister and I all reach for more popcorn. Temples and crowded bridges, rivers and hazy mountains flash up on our empty wall. My mother notices something on a temple, a bit of fresco peeking out behind a man with nothing on. Yes, I was just trying to get that for you, dear, says my father, when that damn guru or whatever came and sat down. The next few slides of the famous temple are obscured by blurred reds and blues. It's a struggle just to get a decent picture, says my father, with all the unwashed masses hanging around. I think about unwashed masses and how India must smell but say nothing. I'm old enough now and know better. There is such a thing, said my father once, as a figure of speech.

The red-eye tour is a bus full of pale damp-faced men in shirt-sleeves and trousers of suits. One or two look better prepared; they wear light cotton shirts and what are called summer-weight pants over here. I do not see my father among these men strolling casually at the base of temples or gazing up into an elephant's eyes. He remains invisible behind the camera; but since India the pictures have changed. He starts to flip through the slides quickly, turning the little wheel on the sliding arm with a loud click, pushing the arm in until the slide drops as if from nowhere on the wall. Then he whips the arm out hard, shooting the slide back into its tray. These were just to use up the film, he says—that was a long day. What we see are snatches of legs, of brown necks and faces. I catch an old woman bent double in a busy street under a basket of wood easily as big as she. A man's surprised face peeks out from an elaborate hole. You wouldn't know it from this picture, says my father, but the carving on that window is as impressive as you'll ever see. He explains that the carving, a peacock with a huge fan, faces out on a dingy little alleyway—you could hardly call it a street. It was carved long ago on the side of this fifteenth century monastery by a man whose hands were later cut off. Or was that another carving in another town? My father is not sure. The peacock represents something, but my father can't remember exactly what. Well, it's certainly lovely, says my mother. She lingers genuinely over the window's details, deriving some pleasure I myself can't sustain. Who's the face in the window? she says. Huh! I don't know, I hadn't noticed him, my father says. I guess, since it's a monastery, it'd be a monk, he laughs, winks conspiratorially at me. My face drains gray, feels incomplete. Somehow, given this wink, I'm not worthy of its receipt.

The peacock window whips away and comes back stuck, jammed with a picture we haven't yet seen. The puzzle-browed man is still gazing through the window, but another face rises through and around him, its huge eyes and mouth containing the wall and window frame. Bugger it, says my father, fiddles with the slide arm, which refuses to release. He touches something, says, There! and looks back at the screen.

But the accident is still there, the double vision. Well, it's the last picture anyway, says my father. It's just a girl who was staring at me on the street.

Centennial Year. We learn a new song in school. For months I sing snatches of this song to myself:
Ca–na–da! We love you!
Ca–na–da! Proud and true!
Hurrah vive-le Canada
Three cheers hip hip hooray
Le centenaire, that's the order of the day!
Frère Jacques, Frère Jacques
Merrily we roll along
Les enfants du pays, Ensemble. . . .

Classes are canceled for a week, and we work on centennial projects. I make a long brown cotton dress with a full skirt and apron, which I imagine looks like the ones ladies wore around 1867. Other girls make fancy print dresses with bows and frills, but I want mine to be authentic; by that I mean slightly dingy, something you could milk a cow in. Night after night I bend over the sewing machine, pulling pins from seams as they slide under the needle's blur. The hem, four yards of it, I sew by hand, a private concession to those unelectric days a hundred years ago. Beyond the shine of my hot fingers under the high-intensity lamp, my mother clicks her tongue: You're crazy, she says, No one cares about a silly hem. I know she's right, it would be better to get my sleep. Instead I ask if it would be all right to use her heavy shawl my father brought back from Spain, and she says, Fine, just don't go and make one, for goodness' sake.

My father is working on a centennial project, too. After dinner he unrolls maps across the living room floor, plucks our wood or glass Scandinavian figurines from their spots on coffee and end tables, lines them up along the sides of the maps to hold them down. Watch out! he calls if I step too near, don't bust your mother's bird! Each map is a section of the Ottawa River, which flows messily over the thick straight paper edges. My father gets excited, jabs at islands and rapids, knocking the glass sentries down. Damn! he swears under his breath and realigns the river, sets the Norwegian owl back on its feet. As the snow browns outside and melts back from the pink granite road in front of our house into the ditches, red marks appear on the maps. There are numbers, 1, 2, up to 11, with circles around them, and large *X*s with other smaller letters—*r* or *s* or *p*—beside them. The numbers, I learn, are the places my father has picked out to camp on the way to Montreal by canoe. The *X*s are rapids he will run or scout or portage. On these spring weekends, my father drives off by himself or with one of us, if he can persuade us it won't be a bumpy throwuppy sort of road. On these excursions, which are always more throwuppy than my father thought, we drive past signs saying PRIVATE PROPERTY – TRESPASSERS WILL BE PROSECUTED, and I divert myself for a few minutes, trying to think how that would differ from PERSECUTED. My sisters have more of a stake in this whole venture, though, than I do; they are going with my father on his centennial project. When we float dizzy and sick out of the car, look down on the roaring rapids and deadheads below and have to shout above the noise to each other to be heard, I am secretly glad there is only room for three in the canoe.

One fog-blind morning in mid-June, I stand beside my mother on the town pier. Others have gathered, too, neighbors and friends, to see my father and sisters off. We don't see much, though, under the mist over the river. My father lifts the canoe from the roof of the car, flips it, slides it down his body—my father, the red canoe, plunging reflections in the smooth water. The fog of mist so damp, so low that we well-wishers hardly see one another. We draw tight; our neighbor shouts over my head—hey Doc (which is what my father calls *him*), you sure this is a good idea? A drop of rain on my cheek, then another. We scramble for hoods, umbrellas, as the sky we can't see spills over our heads. My father flips up the hoods on my sisters squall jackets, says, Are you warm enough? Put a sweater on, for God's sake! Back and forth from the car—and now there are offers of help—my father pulls ancient canvas packs, paddles, sponges, bailing cans, a sheet they will use for a sail when the wind favors them. Everything disappears into plastic—my father has come prepared with green garbage bags—and is loaded into the canoe. He tells my middle sister to sit in the center of the canoe, and they pack bags around her so she can't move. She smiles up at me and shrugs; I giggle and ripple my fingers back. Then my father hands my oldest sister a paddle and holds the gunwale against the dock while she climbs down into the bow. Then he comes and gives me a quick damp hug and my mother a bare kiss and goes back to the edge of the pier and steps off. And now all of us are caught in this muggy scene— we on the shore waiting for the warmth of houses, my father and sisters in suspension on the river, three gray monks under the cold rain. The wind is beginning to pick up, the water is not silver anymore but chopped up black, fragmented. How much freeboard ya got there? someone shouts and my father grins. About six inches or so, he says. Not to worry, Mac, we could run a hurricane with that! And then my father tells my oldest sister to push off with her paddle from the dock. Forward ho! he says, when my sister's paddle hesitates over the choppy water. Goodbye! Good luck! Have fun! Be careful! we shout. WHOOPS! says my father when my sister's paddle gets stuck for a moment and the canoe rocks perilously. Caught a crab already! he shouts merrily, but we barely hear him through the mist. Or we hear him clearly but hardly see, the sharp red freshly painted curve of the cedar-strip lost and found and lost again in the climbing water. The last thing I see as the canoe disappears is my father's paddle lifted high over his still forward-looking head, waving to us back on shore a signal we are expected to read.

What are you going to do with your life? my father asks me at fifteen. I am carrying laundry down the stairs to the basement. It's a good question I've been considering for some time. His asking, however, does not bring any one answer forward in my mind. In fact the more I think about this question, the more it becomes like those trick or bonus questions teachers put at the end of exams. Some of my fellow students drift against these questions with glee—they are the ones who slide up to me afterward in the hall, ask, What did you get for number 19? then look falsely surprised when I say I didn't get past 15.

What are you going to do with your life? This question leaves me feeling chilled. There's a transference, an inversion required, that I can't make. What have I ever *done* with my life? Nothing to which I could point specifically, tell a stranger, I did that. Sure there are actions I've taken—sneaking a bottle of rum into the Strand with my best friend; playing bright but unpopular Esther three years ago in the school play; collecting UNICEF, when I was younger, at Halloween—but these no longer seem clearly accomplished in the context of this larger problem. What does a life look like? What color is it? Is its texture smooth or rough? What does it sound like—a hum, a jaunty tune perhaps, a deep bass drum? How does a life smell: rotting leaves, diesel, fresh-cut pine? And taste? If I had this object, my life, here in my hand, bestowed as a gift from someone who asked merely that something be *done* with it, what would I do? *What will I do?*

I think I might like to write. (Not long ago my father knocked on my bedroom door. Knock! he said loudly and came in. I turned from the poem on my desk, and he turned red, stammered, I—I'm sorry, backed out and closed the door.) Good luck, my dear, he says, and flicks his paper, I hope you find someone rich to support you. Someone, I know, means some man. This man is as real or unreal to me as anything in the world I choose to ponder. He is as generous or cold as a foreign city.

Where am I now? Turning away, continuing down to the basement with the laundry. When the basket crashes to the floor, and I collapse on top of it unexpectedly, throat aching, tears dribbling inadequately over the dirty sheets. I can't see, I keep saying, I can't see, which is true. I've taken you halfway around the bloody world, says my father, what more do you need to see?

Rot! Gelb! Blau! Grün! Grau! Braun! Rot! Gelb! Blau! Grün! Grau! Braun! Herr Mann strides across the front of the classroom, pointing at blotches on a white posterboard. It's my first German class. The idea now is you are not to speak English when learning a foreign language. Rot! Gelb! Blau! Grün! Grau! Braun! It sounds like a sort of rhyme to me, and the blotches are like beats; I am the last in the class to understand these sounds refer to the colors of the blotches. I think about Helen Keller, blind-deaf-dumb, holding her hands under the water while Teacher alternately pumped and spelled W-A-T-E-R onto Helen's palm. I picture Helen Keller as she was before Teacher (I've seen the Walt Disney movie), crashing around her house in disorderly fits, jamming food into her mouth like an animal. And then Teacher, who spelled WATER on her palm. It seems a miracle all right, so much that the deeper I think into this miracle, the more unlikely it seems. Sometimes I close my eyes, try to imagine not hearing or speaking; it would be like being buried alive. The only senses left: smell and touch. If something cold and wet kept jumping on my hands and running down, if someone kept banging on my palm at the same time—would I make the connection? Or would I think it was just another soul trapped in the same box as me, thinking *I* was the way out?

Graduation. Official marks are not yet in for Grade Thirteens, but unofficially we've all passed. Better—many of us are Ontario Scholars. We know already we are stars. We sit in the crêpe-papered dining hall, while the principal, certain enthusiastic teachers and the valedictorian make their speeches. Brassieres can be seen poking out from spaghetti straps; some of the boys have loosened their ties.

This morning, on my last exam—World Religions—I got to the bonus question. It was an obscure reference to the *Upanishads,* the ancient Hindu texts. Already we'd had a short-answer question: Hindus believe in two possible paths the devotee can take. One of these is called the Northern Way. Describe briefly and show how it leads to enlightenment. The Northern Way, I wrote, is also called the Way of the Gods. It eschews outward action (exclusive performance of sacrifices, deeds or penances) for inward contemplation. Meditation on certain forms, known as the five fires, leads the devotee gradually to liberation from mundane illusion; he comes to know the Supreme Self by becoming one with Brahman, the absolute and unchanging cosmic vital force. Then came the bonus question. In the *Upanishads,* reference is made to the five fires. What are they? I knew them, I knew all five, but when the time was up, I couldn't remember the last one. Heaven, the Rain God, This World, Woman and _____. *Man.* I knew it, I knew it. But what will count is what I got down. Heaven, the Rain God, This World, Woman. Four out of five.

After the speeches there is dessert. Then the parents and

teachers go home. I float downstairs with the other girls (the boys are somewhere behind). Peach voile, pink taffeta, we ripple over the music flowing up from the lounge for the dance.

I am not alone in my new home. A housefly struggles absurdly across the white page I write on, under the hot study lamp my mother bought before I came to university. The light is never good enough in those places, she said, when I protested the fuss. You can always use more. My assignment is for a course I am taking, the Philosophy of Morals. Its title, chosen from three possibilities on a stencilled sheet the professor gave out, is Do I Have the Moral Right to Kill Myself? I am arguing in the affirmative and am nearly done.

I follow the fly across the page with my pen for a while, then drop the nib in front of its nose (possible essay topic: Do Flies Have Noses?) Why doesn't it fly away? I look closer and see the fly hop up, spin around, land backward on the paper. It only has one wing. Again I drop the pen. I'll give this half-dead bug a reason to live, I say to myself, something to overcome. And the fly does seem to perk up, it darts left, right, as I lower and lower what must seem to it a formidable and stubborn barricade. I wonder if it wonders what it's up against. Probably not, I decide, its movements are just reflex, a natural response. I squash that slow life with my hand, take up the essay with new vigor.

Falling into this scene, a single shout—male, guttural . . . hopeful. I lean, lift the heavy curtain aside. The bare blast of January window. This is Montreal, after all, no warmer than home, the thirty-below city frigid, steaming. Now other blacknesses lift around me; skewed triangles of light appear one by one in the sides of the adjacent buildings. Three, four, five voices whip the night. Then silence. Rows upon rows of silhouettes, single student residents outlined in yellow light.

We stand utterly still, blank penitents before what we don't need to confirm are the Northern Lights. Aurora borealis. What other name could there be for this brilliant sea, this vast, buoyant, throbbing green?

December. Taste of snow in the air. At Dorchester station, purring diesel. I move among the buses' warm flanks, peer into their split silver bellies. At one I pause and a hard pinching hand overcomes mine on the grip. The driver swings the grip, my pack, slides them along the ridges of the floor. Next! he yells, but I am not ready to move on, stand frozen before the gaping hole. My red backpack swallowed under leather, vinyl, more leather, a cloth bag like a laundry sack. Only when my baggage disappears do I hurry forward, step up into the stale reek of the bus door.

My sisters are not home yet from their cities for Christmas, so my father and I go out alone to find a tree. I'll find something to do here, says my mother when I ask if she's coming and winks Santa-wise at me.

Our tires plough snow up a narrow bush road. When we get to a likely spot, my father runs the car into a snowbank, in case someone wants to get by. Here, he says, handing me the saw. I'm going to take these. The binoculars, he means, in case of interesting birds.

Are you coming on the bird count this year? my father asks when I'm sixteen. I hesitate. The bird count is getting up before light one day in the Christmas holidays, driving along frozen bush roads in pitch black to the town dump, counting crows, shaking a frozen pen till it writes and marking the sighting on a chart. There is a group that does this every year, drives around the back roads into clearings my father knows about, along power lines, across ponds frozen solid, dark. I went once when I was eleven or so, but the birds were asleep that year. THEW! he made a noise with his tongue on the roof of his mouth—not a blessed bloody thing. A few sparrows and finches, one loo–oo–one pine grosbeak on old McKay's back lot. Well, here, get some soup in you, said my mother. You both look frozen stiff.

I stall about the bird count until my father says, Well, I guess that means you're not. But I am awake in the dark Christmas Eve morning when my father pads past my bedroom down the stairs in his triple-stockinged feet. Soon after, I hear those feet, which have acquired heavy boots, crunch on the frozen driveway under my window. The car engine requires a few starts to turn over but then whines quickly and quietly off.

It's as though we're walking on air. Our steps are silent, bottomless, the snow filling in around our feet. You still doing the bird count? I say. It's tomorrow, he says, and then, as though I've said or thought something unkind, I'm *sorry*, it was the only time we could all get together. Maybe I'll come, I say. My father looks surprised. You don't want to leap up at the crack of dawn and freeze to death, surely, he says. There's not much around to see this year. What's it for anyway, I say, I never did find out. What? says my father. The bird count, what's it for? It started down in the States, says my father, back before the turn of the century. It's spread all over North America now. They compile the statistics and publish them every year. Do they do anything with them? I say. Sorry? says my father. Do they do anything with the statistics, like figure out if pollution's killing them off or whatever? Nah! says my father. Just publish them, year by year.

All this time my father has been lifting the binoculars to his eyes, then putting them down. Does your father always do that? a friend once asked me back in high school. Do what? I said. Look away through the binocs when you're talking to him. This was a surprise. I couldn't imagine my father not scanning the sky. Driving, eating breakfast, walking along a street, his light blue eyes would jerk up constantly, filing bird names and sightings in his head, noting a particular cloud configuration or diseased branches on the local trees. I took this attention to the surrounding atmosphere for granted. It did not seem rude or strange to me.

How about that one, I say, pointing to a potential Christmas tree. My father mumbles under his breath. What? I say, tromping over to the tree. Terrible scruffy, says my father, too loud this time, but he laughs. He hardly seems to have looked, already the binoculars are glued back on his eyes. If I had said that, he would have corrected: Terrib*ly*. I ignore him, knock snow off the branches energetically, circle the tree. He's right. Half the branches are dead, one side is almost bare. Okay, okay, I say. When we've walked a bit farther, my father veers off into denser bush. I follow him, stepping over deadfall, ducking around eye-level twigs. He lets a branch go prematurely, and a huge clump of snow lands on my neck. WHOOP! he says. Watch out! as though this cold trickle were my fault. His arm plunges into the center of a tree, and he shakes the whole thing by the trunk. Whaddyathinkofthat, he says, stepping back. It's a nice tree, I say. Here, he says, gimme dat. His hand is held out. I pass him the saw, and the next thing I know he is on his stomach in the snow, sawing away at the bottom of the tree. I move in and hold the top so it doesn't fall on my father's head. After a while my father slides back on his knees—how would you like to give your old man a rest, he says, and offers me the saw. For my father this is a softening, but I have learned not to be caught out. I take the saw, lie down in the basin he has made in the snow and fit the saw back in his groove. You got the tree? I ask. Just saw, dear, says my father, leave the tree to me. The groove my father has made is too deep, the saw bites, then sticks in the raw wound. Start in from the other side, then, says my father, before we bloody well freeze to death.

The chill we both expected. But something is different. (My father is clapping his gloved hands and shaking his jowls.) Something is different about us—but I can't think about that now. I line up the saw on the bark on the other side of the trunk and push hard to get it to bite in. A jerky start, then the saw begins to slide freely, back and forth, fine yellow falling on the white snow below. My arms ache, but I feel triumphant, the saw singing, This way, that way, this way, that way, as it glides in and out by itself. How ya doing down there, says my father, meaning the tree should have toppled long ago. I stop sawing and look; my groove angles up over my father's, they cross without meeting. Well, get outa there, he says. I'll push it down. I scramble away from the base just as my father kicks the trunk. Timber! he says. Now, who's going to drag it back to the car? In the end, he does, of course, he's brought a rope along in his pocket. I half-walk, half-run behind with the binoculars and saw.

I'm as drunk as I've ever been, the kind of drunk you get once and are always trying for again. I am swaying back and forth, my arms crossed in front of my chest, holding hands with two strangers. We are singing in a German beer garden in English a song I learned a lifetime ago in public school:

Have you ever seen a lassie
Go this way and that way . . .
Have you ever seen a lassie
Go this way and that?

I do not question the English as I am singing, only know I can now join in easily, after a number of songs slip away.

I'm taking a year off university to travel around Europe. So far I've been to England, France and Italy on my student Eurail pass. Now I'm heading north again. I got off the train this morning in Bavaria, and already I qualify for the postcard I mailed home this afternoon, showing a laughing group of friends under an Oktoberfest banner. As we sing, someone taps me on the shoulder. I turn. A man stands behind me with a complicated camera. Rolls of film, a collapsed tripod, extra lenses dangle awkwardly from his shoulders. Bitte, he says to me and continues in fast German. I barely hear him over the oom-pah and my caroling neighbors, but the beer helps, and I understand him perfectly. Will I ask my friends if they would pose for a postcard photo? I smile, beckon him closer. He puts a freckled ear next to my mouth. These aren't my friends! I yell in English. I'm not from here! The man's brow folds, then he moves off down the table to a loud burly patron, unmistakably local. Soon, under the guidance of the photographer and the local, we are pretending to do what we were doing before the photographer arrived. But now we hold our glasses higher, swing farther, look in each other's eyes.

I am in love with my history professor. But this does not prevent my becoming the object of others' affection. Of these mistaken Romeos, an acquaintance from my year in Europe writes suddenly from Stettler, Alberta, a town I've never heard of. I gather this place is what my father would call the back of beyond. It took me awhile to track down your address in Montreal, he writes, but if I don't get this letter back from the post office like all the others, I'll know I've finally got it right. I crumple up the letter, fire it down the hall into a basketball hoop my co-op roommates have erected on the front door for my use. Two more points for me! I shout. You girls don't have a hope! The next day I get another letter from Stettler. It begins: Damn it, last night I couldn't sleep. I walked around the goddamn frozen tundra for hours under the stars, thinking of you. I crumple and shoot, hit the rim, then it bounces through. Another two! I yell, although everyone is out.

The next day when I come home from class, he is waiting at the top of the cold walk-up staircase, his breath making humped otters in the air. He is bigger than I remember, round and broad-backed and bearded. He looks like a bush pilot, which is what he is. It took him three days to get here in the twin-engine, he says. Can he take me out for dinner? We walk down to old Montreal, there's a restaurant he's heard about. We find it and go in. The restaurant is nothing special, a slightly expensive mock-up of old France, with new French waiters in tuxedos. My companion suggests we start with escargots, and I don't object, since it's on his bill. I can't see him all that well in the flicker of the candle, but his lips glisten under his beard, from butter or saliva or both, I can't tell.

Now I have a déjà vu. And then I see it is not a déjà vu, this *has* all happened before. I was staying at the youth hostel in Paris, which seemed a pigsty, a dump—even to me. When a Dane came in drunk one night and threw up on my bed, I moved to a hotel. I handed my room key in to the hostel warden and turned heavily under my backpack to leave. I heard a kind of clicking, which I ignored until I was about to open the front door to leave. There it was again, only louder, more insistent. Somehow I knew this clicking, whatever it was, was meant for me. I turned, and there was the hostel warden clicking his tongue through his split front teeth. A white drop of spittle ran sideways along the rim of his lip, unnoticed by him but obvious to me. It seemed he knew where I was going, not on to the next city but just down the street. My lip twisted sheepishly, I tried to think of some excuse. But he started to talk in textbook French before I could get a word in. Going down to Mme Thibeault's, was I? Felt the need of a break? A break from a holiday? Well, it made sense. Even tourists—true?—have their ups and downs. He phrased everything as a question, which he then answered, boring through me with his eyes. Boring me, I see now, but then I thought he saw everything inside.

I'd been twenty-four hours at Mme Thibeault's pension when the first quiet note slipped under my door. In easy tempting French, the French I'd learned at school, which back home was of no use, it said, Coffee today about four. And named a place. No questions there. The note was anonymous, but I had no doubt. Of course I didn't meet him. I took to stealing from my room at odd hours, in semidisguises, hoping he had posted no lookouts.

But I didn't move on to another hotel, either, which I could easily have done. And when, a few days later, a thin bottle of expensive perfume slid under my door, I was not inclined to push it back through. Instead I put on my only dress (pink), lavished the perfume heavily on some pulse spots I'd heard about, flung open the front door of the hotel and walked out.

The truth was, my money was low; I had not expected to still be in Paris when I'd wired home a week before. By now the pension had drained me almost completely, and until I got back to London, there was no hope of more dough. I'd been living on cheap wine and bread and cheese, as travelers do, but that was getting old. I felt the need of a solid meal. I drifted down the street, past the open hostel door. I was about to turn around for a second flyby, when I heard the waited-for sound. *TKKK-TKKK, TKKK-TKKK!* I peered in to the front desk through the door. Mademoiselle, Mademoiselle! chanted my Parisian, Ma petite Canadienne errante! And he asked me for dinner, just like that. Non, non! I insisted. C'est trop, trop! Trop, trop? he said. Ah, ma petite errante. Tu es n'est-ce pas bien amusante!

That evening we went to the best restaurant in the district, where he dropped quick pellets of French, like speed, into my ears. His phrases grew quicker and quicker, his little questions more numerous, as the evening drew on. When there was time, I threw in a oui or non, either of which would send him off again, to make some point anew. After dinner he asked me up to his apartment. You must be kidding, I said in English, and left him babbling at the foot of his stairs.

The bush pilot is not like this. Despite the snooty French restaurant, the candles, the penguin waiters, the escargots, he is slow, deliberate, English. He tells me he's been studying ballet to discipline his body; he's into Zen and meditation and yoga and reads Yukio Mishima, who is an inspiration. Well, good, I say, good for you, but I don't know what to say after that.

Later I tell my roommates about the bush pilot who is into Zen. They blow on their fingers and shake them exaggeratedly, they roll their eyes and say, She's done it again. Seriously though, I say, what do you think? Seriously, they say, you're crazy to let him get away. Which is what I have done. I stood on the runway like an old movie and waved to the tiny cockpit head. What about the fact he's two years younger than me? I say. They shake their heads. Really? they say. Well, he's good for a few years yet then, eh? But I wasn't, well, *attracted* to him, I say. They dangle their legs over our beanbag chairs, flip the pages of books they are reading. Besides, my heart is spoken for, I say. I only went to dinner with the guy 'cause he came all that way. Shoot yourself, they say brightly, crackling bags of cheezies on their knees. I will, I say, I will suit myself.

I pull on coat, hat, boots, mitts and scarf and flounce down the outside stairs to the street. Those girls, my roommates, are just jealous of my catch. I stomp, head down, along the sloping sidewalks, past the laundromat (known unofficially as Dirty Joe's), past the secondhand bookstore called The Word, which in a few years will be officially transfigured as Le Mot. Past the student coffee house, The Yellow Door, which is just that. My stomach is starting to buzz, which means I am getting close to my love. In fact he lives only two streets over.

The old attached brick building resembles ours. But inside, the story is very different. It has been gutted, repainted, stripped back to the original wood floors. Unlike most people I know, my history professor-lover does not like wood floors. Why do you want a hard floor? he says. That's what carpets were *invented* for! He neglects them deliberately, makes large black scuffs, which he refuses to clean up. Give me a carpet any day, he says, wall-to-wall shag with a good underlay. He says it's no coincidence that with the sexual revolution came the pill and the shag rug. Spontaneity is the key.

In my own apartment at night, I watch cockroaches scatter under the kitchen light and think of those wood floors. Neglected, yes, but even their latent beauty cheers me. It's comforting to know the renovation wave has come this far. Yeah, right, say my roommates, when I express this optimism, you got a few hundred thousand bucks? We'll have to move out. They're right. When the wave reaches us, we will either have to renovate or move out.

My professor's house is spacious, warm, but there is only one old couch, a yellowed foam mattress, a TV, stereo, nothing as yet on the walls. I've only been here a year, he grins, gathers me into his arms. It's . . . got . . . potential we say to each other between kisses. We are pretending each kiss gives us the strength to go on. I bury my head in the moth-eaten shoulder of his sweater. The wool is scratchy, his long hair tickles my cheek. But he holds me tight against him, and I do not move.

My father is off to Vienna to work at the UN. He's there now, looking for a place to live. My mother stays behind to pack up the house, which will be rented out while they are gone. Classes are over, I'm a graduate, so I go home to help.

When I get there, the packing is just about done. In the morning we wrap up the crystal glasses, the good china, the Norwegian figurines in newspaper and tuck them in cardboard boxes they've been saving for my mother at the A&P. In the afternoon it is too hot to work, and we sit in the screened porch, protected from the blackflies just beginning to appear. My mother sips iced tea, looks at me. I am looking at her, our eyes catch, we smile quickly and turn away. I get up, restless, walk over with my cup to the screen and look out.

My father walks up the street when I'm fourteen, in his brown suit and heavy shoes with the swirls and holes for decoration on the toes, carrying his briefcase. On the step he puts down the briefcase, flips the soft leather tab, opens its yawning mouth. Takes something out. At first it looks like a black butterfly net. But he fits it over his head, a solid piece that sits on top with a ring of hard rubber like a hoop that holds it out in a circle from his face. The door squeals and he walks in. My mother is in the kitchen at the sink—a direct line from the front door. Hello, dear! calls my father as usual when he comes home from work. The next thing I hear is my mother's scream. My father and I laugh, and I bounce off the couch and beg to try the contraption on. Give it to your mother, he says. She might as well get used to it now.

The special bug helmets, whose black screens fall to the shoulder from the brim, are for a canoe trip they are taking, he says, to Moosonee. All winter long we watch, amused, as my father spins out his latest dream. Then we are caught in it ourselves; around us the house and yard are filling with dried food, new paddles, rain ponchos, mysterious maps—artifacts of adventure, my father's vision of a promised land.

The morning my parents are to leave, I wake to the sound of a recorder—a march. I wash my face, stroll sleepily downstairs. My father, clad in his tartan housecoat, is high-stepping a circuit around the main floor of the house. I can see the end of the recorder but not his face. On my father's shoulders sits the bug helmet, his head as darkly bulbous as the man from Mars.

When my mother is ready to fly overseas, I meet her at Mirabel Airport. I see her, but she still does not see me. She wears a beige all-weather coat—looks new, I think—and lugs two large suitcases. Her purse is tucked under her arm. She looks around nervously at other passengers, the television screens with long lists of scheduled flights. Her cheeks are beginning to wrinkle quite a lot—something she is self-conscious about. I caught her pulling up her skin in front of the mirror when I was home and said, You're crazy, they just add character. That did not comfort her.

I walk up to my mother just as she is turning back the other way and wrestle all her bags into my arms. I'm not an invalid, she says, I can carry something, dear. No, no it's all right, I say, although it isn't.

We drink coffee in a smoke-filled cafeteria, waiting for her flight. My mother says, Is there something on your mind, dear? No, I say. What makes you think that? You just seemed quiet. There's nothing on my mind, Mother, okay? But my mother does not look away; she has come armed, determined about something. I noticed you were reading Jung when you were home. Yeah, we took it in psychology, I said, but I never had time then. A lie—I'm reading it again. It's a good book, she says, and I soften. *The Undiscovered Self,* as far as I'm concerned, is the supreme analysis of everything that is wrong with this world. Don't swallow it whole, though, says my mother; at the same moment, her flight is called. Better get you down there, I say. You wouldn't want to miss your flight. On the bus back downtown from the airport, I'm angry, puzzled about what she said. I open the book—I carry it with me in my purse—and re-read the publisher's blurb inside the front cover: "Only when the individual understands the duality of his nature—his capacity for evil as well as for good—can he begin to understand and cope with the potential threat of those in power." The idea seems obvious to me, already absorbed, almost outdated. I cannot fathom my mother's caution.

That winter my roommates kick me out. We like you, like you *a lot*, they say, but let's face it, you're a slob. It's true. I can't remember ever cleaning the toilet bowl or bathtub, dusting or vacuuming the rug. Everything they accuse me of is undeniable—I put it down to a high tolerance for dirt and a mother who did all the cleaning up. Well, goodbye, I say to them, I'm sure I'll see you soon. It will be unavoidable, I mean, since I'm just moving two streets up. Nothing much to clean at History's house, I say as a parting gesture, hoping to cheer them. (History is what I've begun to call my professor, a lover's joke.) When I stumble across his threshold laden with packsack, suitcase, small grip, shoulder bag and purse, and fall onto the moth-eaten shoulder, pouring tears into the ragged holes, he reaches for the tea towel I brought and tells me to lift my head.

By day I work in the alumni office of the university, writing cheery letters to generations of ex-students, encouraging donations to their alma mater. Dear _____, I write, I hope this long hot summer finds you and your family relaxed, cool and refreshed. Summer is a time for slowing down, reading a book or two, taking stock. A time to make new acquaintances and remember old friends. And speaking of old friends . . .

My father is on this faceless list. When his name comes up, the typist asks if I've got anything to add to the letter. Naw, not today, I say. I'll slip a note in when the magazine goes out. Then one of these letters comes back, a magazine, another letter. The tenants in our house must be sick of this stuff, I think. One day the typist says to me, We seem to have lost your father. They've moved to Vienna, I say, as though they're never coming back. The office staff are disappointed: it's always been fun reading his return letters. They dig out his last one: Dear Alumnicks, he had written, Up here in the back country, as you may know, summer is neither long nor unbearably hot (the blackflies will eat you alive, though, if you don't watch out), and if I weren't getting up every morning to go to work to earn some money to support my family and all the hardworking citizens of this country who feel it necessary to relax and refresh themselves on UIC for the summer, I would be pleased to ease myself down on a lawn chair with a tall drink and join the nirvanic millions who have found the secret to keeping cool in the throes of the punishing Canadian summer. . . .

Still my father would always enclose a smallish cheque, which, after all, say my co-workers, was better than nothing. I'll take his name off the list, then, shall I? says the typist. He didn't send us a change of address. I guess he won't want to be bothered over there. I shrug. I received their new address some weeks ago on a postcard from my mother, but I do not tell my co-worker that. Something I can only describe as hopelessness curls over me; I feel tired, indolent, slightly dazed.

I am not thinking about my father anymore but of History, our life together. I picture the way we will be tonight when I go home, like every other night, snuggled together on his battered hardwood floor. We will not talk much. He will listen to the news on the radio, switch to the TV, back to the radio for the after-news current affairs on CBC. It's his job, he says, to know what's going on in the world. Once or twice during commercials I will wonder aloud about my parents, my sisters, my best friend Robin, what they're doing now. I might even cry a little, for no reason. What's wrong, he will say, and put his arm around me. But then the commercial will be over and a landslide in Peru that has killed thousands will make this small riffle on the smooth evening seem trivial even to me. You think you've got problems, he will say, and smile.

History writes papers, publishes books with regularity: "Uneasy Democracy: Internal Struggle in the Irish Republic Army"; "Aftershock in Vietnam"; "Loves Labor's Lost in the United Kingdom" (my title suggestion); *The European Economic Community and COMICON: Ten Years in the Life.* Meetings are taking up more and more of his time now. Whenever the word committee is mentioned, he rolls his eyes. Can't you decline some of them? I suggest. Not if I volunteer, he says. Out-of-town scholars and in-town, poor graduate students begin to appear for dinner, for breakfast. They stay for a day or a week, sometimes longer. Couldn't some of them stay in a hotel? I say. They'd be more comfortable, wouldn't they? It's so impersonal, says History. You know how you feel in a foreign city. And I can't argue with that. Besides, says History, you don't need to look after them. Just show them the kitchen and let them at it. Okay, I say, but they always ask where we keep the table and chairs. They'll just have to sit on the floor like we do, says History. If they can't sit on the floor, they don't have to come. My father would call this Women's Logic, but I don't tell History that.

My office has a generous summer holiday plan—you can take two weeks with pay or two months without. I make spontaneous outrageous plans during the winter to keep our spirits up. How about cycling around Ireland, I suggest, or Scotland, where my ancestors are from? How about hiking in the Alps? How about living in a yurt in Tibet? How about flying to the moon? We settle for bicycling around Ireland. History says that's best for him since there's some Irish history he wants to look up. He probably can wangle some money from the university, he says, or take it out of his research grant. I buy an atlas and open it in front of us at night. I get excited then, run my fingers over possible routes. I want to go there, I say. Where? says History. The Knock-meal-down Mountains, I say. Doesn't it sound great? Whatever you say, says History, but don't forget we don't have bicycles yet.

In the end we spend the summer in Montreal. A conference comes to town that History is chairing, then some more scholars and students. Maybe I'll go visit my folks in Vienna, I say over the war in the Middle East one evening. Kind of late, isn't it? says History, You'll have to pay full fare. Sure enough, when I phone Air Canada, it will cost nearly a thousand dollars. If I'd booked back in April, there was a special to Frankfurt.... Oh, no, I say, thank you, it's Vienna I'm interested in. Thanks anyway. That night when I relay this news to History, he looks momentarily grieved. But I notice, as he takes a shower, he is singing, You can't go home again.... Maybe I'll go visit Robin in Toronto, I say the next day. Surely we can afford that. Sure, says History, go ahead. I hear it was over thirty degrees Celsius there yesterday and the pollution index was ninety-one.

It's arranged. I'm going to take the VIA Turbo to Toronto and spend the August long weekend with my friend. That Thursday I come down with a summer flu. History comes home from his office in the afternoon and finds me fetal and blubbering on our foam bed. What's wrong, he says, kisses me on the forehead. But my tongue is incapable of movement, it is taut, pulled back in my open mouth as far as it can go. If I release it, the house will come crashing down. It's just a fever, says History, a lot of my students have it. I think there's some penicillin someone left in the bathroom. Here, he says, handing me some pills and a glass of water. Get some sleep.

The next morning when I wake up, I look over and History is gone. He's learned to shut off the alarm before it starts, after I complained about waking up to the news. I lie on my back, focus on a small dirt mark on the ceiling, gathering the strength to get up. When I do, I walk carefully to the bathroom, so as not to provoke dizziness. I sit on the toilet for a long time, get up and wash my face in the basin with some Pears soap someone left, pat dry with exaggerated movements. I shuffle into the kitchen and slowly, slowly begin to make pancakes, which I have not eaten, it seems, for years. This breakfast making is like a dream. I pause between each ingredient, trying to remember what my sisters and I used to do. I have to visually picture the flour in a cup measure, the baking powder in a tablespoon. I must reenact bending down to get the sifter from under my mother's counter, though there is no sifter here. Gradually I build the batter until it seems about the right consistency. As the pancakes sputter in the frying pan, everything becomes clearer. My eyes are still runny, I can't see as well as I should, but the floor and walls are perpendicular again, even the TV is losing its double edge.

In the spring, layers of dog excrement are exposed like geological strata under the warming sun. I saunter home from work, kicking a stone, the object to keep it rolling as long as possible while dodging unsavory smears on the cement. I am not unhappy; looking up at green-fringed trees, smelling damp grass, I see that the Montreal spring is a thing of beauty. It seems there is some kind of plan after all and, further, that I am not omitted from this plan.

The apartment door is unlocked when I arrive—unusual—and I step into the hall. Several windows must be wide open, the door slams shut behind me. Then History pops from the kitchen doorway like an apparition. He is waving something in his hand, airline tickets. He steps in front of me, blocking my way, then folds his arms around my neck. Guess where we're going, he says, his eyes darting over my shoulder, as though not to lose sight of the tickets. Ireland? I say. East Germany? Try again, he says. Vienna? Baghdad? Saigon? None of the above, he says triumphantly. Now he can't stop himself. Nepal! he cries. No expression fits my face. I feel several come and go. Prompt! I shout, to show spirit. For a second, History's face clouds, he doesn't get my meaning. Himalayas! he blurts. Mt. Everest! God-kings! Temples! And now I see it, too, I feel spring air rush through the open windows against my face, around my neck. Sacred cows! Living goddesses! Shangri-la!

Shangri-la. My arms now flung on History's neck. *Shangri-la.* Just assure me of one thing, I say (we dance dizzily around the kitchen floor). What's that? asks History, laughing. No alumnicks in Shangri-la, I say. No alumni in Shangri-la, he says. I do solemnly swear.

That night we lie sweatily apart in bed, insomniac from lovemaking. History's arms are folded behind his head, he has flung the covers to the foot of the bed to cool off. But why? I say. Why what? Why Nepal? I say. History explains. It's the only place in living memory where they've kicked out a prime minister and reinstalled a king. I stare into the dark, then turn my face to the window just in time to catch the raccoon that lives on our back alley garbage staring back. The first time I saw the raccoon, I was thrilled and frightened, told the story, beefed up, at History's department parties, to amuse his colleagues, whom I took to be our friends. Now these sightings are a common occurrence we don't even mention to each other. The raccoon turns its body heavily and slumps down out of sight. I've signed us up for a rock-climbing course, says History. They say it's all a mind game. I figure if we're going to go to Everest, we should do it right.

After the first climbing class, the world will not lie down. The doctor calls it vertigo, as though the condition were mine, but I perceive a troubled topography in which roads, people, houses flip up on their sides. Trees, buildings, light standards whirl around me. This whizzing is not frightening but rather an intriguing, purposeful confusion, not malicious but effective, experimental, even compassionate in some way I do not yet understand.

When the next class comes up, I hand History his helmet and pack. Climb well! I shout cheerily over the klump of his hiking boots on the stairs. When the outside door of the apartment latches behind him, I walk calmly, so calmly through the blur. Fridge, stove and broom closet wheel like white birds around me. They dive and veer, straining my balance. But I reach the drawer where I saw him put the envelope, open it up and look in. There it is. *With compliments from Mystic Travel* and a telephone number. I remove my ticket and replace the envelope in the drawer. Sitting down by the phone, I dial the number I saw on the envelope's corner.

"Mystic Travel."

I explain my reason for calling, and the nasal voice says, "One moment please."

Moments become minutes that in turn drag on. Finally the clipped adenoidal reply: "Yes. And the date you wish to go?"

I am stunned, literally taken aback. The wall beside me has suddenly reared up, nudging me from the arm of the couch into its cushions. This is too easy, too guilt free, too spare. "This time next week?" The voice begins quotations from six A.M. on.

"No, I mean *this time,* do you have something, say, between seven and nine?"

They do. It is all arranged, with only a small extra fee for changing departure dates.

"I'll just put it on the account, then, shall I?" the voice says. And I say that will be fine.

Will we be flying over Vienna at all? I ask History when he

comes home that night. If one were going as the crow flies, he says, but there's no such thing as a direct flight to Kathmandu. We'll have to land in Rome first after London (there's something he's researching about the Italian Renaissance), then Delhi and finally Kathmandu.

I know about these stops of course, I've looked at the ticket, but I want to hear it from him. That night I sleep deeply. Toward morning I dream of drowning. The water is clear with a blue tint, the fish friendly, curious. My lungs fill, something inside me like a secret moving, then I am on the other side. Like that. I'm still thinking and watching. I still have eyes. So this is what it's like to be dead, I say. Then I wake up.

I walk to work, a bright scene lambent on a dark unexplored sea. A nightmare. Something I have done. This thing is like stealing a ticket, but worse. The ticket, after all, was meant for me—I only rearranged the dates for a small fee. The cheque my father sent in the envelope with my mother's postcard was not for me. It said very clearly the name of the university. Clearly to me. Most people can't read my father's cramped writing, but I know it intimately. I spent lazy hours as a kid forging his signature innocently on blank pieces of paper, more hours when I was older, not so innocent, on notes of absence from unsavory events at school. A large amount. More than my father had ever donated before.

It is the first time I've thought, really thought, about the details of what I've done. At the time it went so smoothly, so quickly. The number I wrote on the sheet was a new account our office had opened, not yet in the computer listings, I told the cashier, and being an old acquaintance, she took my word. I had come at a busy time; she had no opportunity then to look it up. What I planned, happened. The money fell out of the uncomputerized ether into an old account I knew about that the office no longer used. The account had been used to pay casual staff we had hired intermittently in the old days, before general efficiency was upgraded. Now all that was needed was to fill out one of the old requisitions still kicking around in my desk. I sent in the form, with my first initial and last name as the payee, and *voilà!* Next payday I walked over to payroll and signed for the cheque I knew already was made out to me.

Today I plan to give notice. No, it's too late for that. I'm leaving next week, I'll have to quit. I only want to think of myself as giving full notice, think of myself as cool, coolly resolved, a successful embezzler strolling away from the perfect crime. Embezzler? Is that what I am now? I am not cool. I feel dizzy again as I walk in the office door and have to sit on a chair and chat to the receptionist to cover my fear. Steady again, I walk past my dingy office to the bright windowed suite occupied by my boss.

Rome isn't so bad, I say. Nor is a free ticket, I'm thinking. I can always go to Vienna another time. I am sharing a bottle of wine with a perfect stranger the first night in my hotel. One thing we have in common: we came on the same flight. We have already tried to find other things in common. The university? I said. No. Montreal? He flew from Toronto and before that, Winnipeg. Vertigo? Is that where everything spins? Yes, I said. As a matter of fact, yes, yes he did, now and then. Vertigo we had in common. But after listing the discomforts and a really amazing sensation he once had, there was not much more to say about it.

It's not Winnipeg, anyway, he says, in response to my comment about Rome. It certainly isn't, I reply. What am I doing staying here with this bore? Then I remember it's my room. It's what he's doing here with me. The time lags in my ticket are all the same as History was planning, just different departure dates. So I am caught here for two days at least. I must plan something to do. I've been here before, of course, on my European tour. So, when the accountant from Winnipeg heads into the mist the next morning, I know exactly where to go. On the way the conversation of last night revisits me. Actually I'm from Gimli, not Winnipeg, he told me, but there's no jobs there. Gimli, I said, isn't that where that airliner went down? I meant the jet forced down in the middle of a trans-Canada flight because it ran out of gas. Yes, he said. That was all. Didn't the pilot glide the plane in, I said, with no engines going at all? Such an incredible thing! Biggest news in Gimli for a thousand years, I'll bet, must be some wild stories there. I suppose so, the accountant said. I never heard them. Didn't you see it or hear it? Didn't you even watch it on the news? Well, I wouldn't hear it, since they glided in, he said. And I guess when the news crews arrived, it was already down.

The Cappella della Pietà in St. Peter's: hushed heart of the world. Before that moving figure, my own body becomes stone. The Madonna, huge and delicate and folded, her crucified son cradled between her thighs in the strong V of her lap. The strained fingers of her right hand support his upper body, hold him to her, while the fingers of her left hand fall open by his knee—pathetic, tender. Head bent, eyes lowered to that lifeless fruit of her womb, the Madonna's face infinite sadness.

But today as I drink in Michelangelo's masterpiece, something overtakes sadness. A strength in the Madonna's draped legs. Her straight back. The soft natural fall of her breasts. I see now that marble can flow up as well as down, lift something, some tiring responsibility. I think of the deranged tourist who walked in and smashed this sculpture to pieces with his fists one day in 1972. He was a mild-mannered tax consultant, they say, who suddenly went berserk. There was speculation he was a frustrated artist, but that was not so.

Then someone claimed to know him, said he'd been under unusual strain. But that turned out to be a sympathetic fellow tourist on the same bus tour who couldn't bear the thought of the man going to jail. In the end no motive was discovered; the last I heard he was undergoing psychological testing to see what they could find out. There are cracks in the Madonna, you can see that, but whether from time or the crazy tourist, it's impossible to tell. Freed suddenly, I turn and leave. On the way back to the hotel, I stop in a café, drink strong, strong coffee deeply.

Delhi, 3 A.M. Desultory sweepers squat, brush-brooms fanning the impossible airport floor. Thickness of crowds, smells, noise. Something wells inside me to equal the surrounding chaos. An exclamation. Nearby passengers glance briefly and turn back to their lives. My light summer dress and sandals squooge with sweat. I wrench my suitcase and backpack from a pile of luggage, make my way slowly through a quick forest of porters' arms to Royal Nepal Air. A tiny lined man with a funny hat stands nervously behind the counter. When I appear (there being no other customers), he smiles widely, shivers his head and disappears through a door. Then just as suddenly, he reappears. Behind him, the most beautiful woman I have ever seen. She speaks softly to the man, then faces me square and expectant. Her nose-jewel catches the light. One ti–cket Kath–man–du, I say slowly. When would you like to fly? says the lady in perfect English. Oh—as soon as possible, I say. The woman consults a ripped sheet of paper for some time. There is more discussion with the truncated man. When—iss—de, says the man carefully, following the woman's finger on the page. Wednesday! I explode. Excuse me, that is the very first flight, says the woman. There are two flights a week only. Well I'll take one for Wednesday then. I pull some Nepali rupees from my money belt. I'm sorry, we don't take. . . . The woman's eyes wander down to my hand. The man points into the seething distance. You will have to change to Indian currency, says the woman. Ow! My hand lands hard against the edge of the counter. I'm trying to stuff the rupees back in my belt, flop a fallen pack back on my shoulder and walk away at the same time. But now the woman's eyes have caught something. Uh . . . one minute miss, she says, as I grapple with my bags. American dollars . . . Yes, yes, I'll pay in American dollars, I say. But there seems to be some hold up. The man and woman behind the counter raise their voices slightly, pull different-looking tickets from their single drawer. Behind them, through an open door, I watch the black sky lighten to gray. Never mind, I say, thanks anyway, I think I'll take the train.

At New Delhi station, I stand for a long time before a closed window, where the man at the next window has directed me to wait. It is 10 A.M. At 12:20, again at the direction of this man, I glance up. A sign over my window announces in four languages including English: 12:30 – 1:30 CLOSED FOR LUNCH. The man wiggle-waggles his head. At 12:25 a beautiful familiar-looking woman works the sticky wooden window up its runners and latches it in place. Her nose-jewel squints, her smile shines past me as though I were a stranger, but I know now this is just a game she plays.

I shut myself into First-Class Air-Conditioned. My bags have arranged themselves (did I hire a porter?) under the seat and along the carriage edges. The train shunts off almost immediately, then stops about a mile down the track, where we now are waiting. I look out the window for the first time with full attention, see children playing. Something is odd, exact, about these children. They throw a stone back and forth to each other. They jump, scream, laugh, run backward with their faces to the sky. And then I see the stone has grown wings. The children are bouncing this bird into the air with a mallet, a racket of some kind. They are playing badminton, but the shuttlecock is alive, flying of its own accord in all directions except where the children sent it. There are no boys among these children, and despite the noise, I see now there are only three. Three pale girls, not Indian children, playing under a gold northern sky. Someone, their mother, walks out on the windy knoll to join them. Girls, it's past midnight! she cries, but the live shuttlecock whirs at her lips, flutters her words away. The woman spins from this nuisance, but the bird spins with her, humming just at her mouth. My mother pirouettes faster and faster, like a skater, until she is only a blur, the tight invisible center of her musical laughter, which spins out higher and higher into the achingly clear arctic air.

And now I am aware of someone else in the carriage. Strange that this awareness has only recently come because he is a large presence, large and leaning. An acrid flavor has filled the compartment. Alcohol of some kind, unidentifiable whiskey. The smell is making me feel ill. The train shunts off again, and the man leans forward in his sallow skin. Would you like something to drink? he says in exquisite English and points to a box on the floor between his legs stamped MILITARY ISSUE ONLY. Anything you like, he says. What'll it be? His phrases don't seem practiced, his accent is perfect, but his language is somehow contrived, as though English is simply a collection of easily memorized clichés. No, no thank you, I say. I look down, away, but when I've waited long enough and glance up at him again to show goodwill, his small black eyes haven't moved from my face. I see that nothing will change until I accept his offer. Well, I say, if you insist (I've never used that phrase before, only heard it in movies), some red wine would be nice. I've stumped him, I think, since Indians, I've heard, are not big on wine. The man leans down, wrenches the wooden lid open with a grunt I am meant to hear. He pulls out a bottle of Bangalore Ruby Red and a long-stemmed glass. As we sip, the man tells me he is going on leave back to his home village in the east. He has traveled alone until my feminine companionship so fortunately befell him. I see now he's been drinking heavily since he got on. I recall the headlines screaming from History's newspaper the night before I left. Some sectarian clashes in outlying areas. This man, I'm sure now, comes from there. When I catch sight of khaki on the rack above his head, the man, who has not taken his eyes from me yet, says, You seem like the type of girl who likes a good story. He tips more wine into my glass, his own, and begins.

It's about a friend of mine, he says. This is a hard-working fellow, mind you. One day he comes home from a long day. He's tired, hungry—he hasn't eaten all day. But his wife, once beautiful, who has let herself go in recent years, is nowhere to be found. Uma! You whore! he calls. Where's my dinner? After many minutes, Uma appears. Her hair is hanging out like a slut, her sari is wrinkled and soiled. Uma! yells my friend. What has happened to you, you look worse than a pregnant leprous bitch! The next day, when my friend comes home from work, again no dinner, and his insolent wife is sitting on the porch step, throwing rice to some crows. My hungry friend must wait nearly till midnight before there is food on his own table! The following night, my friend comes home from work as usual, again no dinner, and his lazy wife is leaning on her elbows on the table, gazing dreamily into a candle flame. Who are you dreaming of, you filthy whore, he says, your cunt-filling dickie who comes to bang you when I am out? (Excuse the coarse language, my dear, I am just translating exactly as it occurred.) Yes, says his wife, he is the one I dream of night and day, especially, it so happens, when you grunt inside me like a dying pig. That is what she said, actually, says my storyteller and shakes his head. My friend, then, understandably filled with rage at such behavior, grabs the candle and yanks his wife upon it by her hair. Once her hair was alight, it was no time until her dress, too, ignited, and my friend's old lady stood aflame before him shrieking like an army of demons all the way down to her well-deserved hell.

The military man smiles across at me. You like that story? he says. You are a sensible good girl. I put my wine glass on the floor so he won't see my hand shaking. The man is laughing now, slapping his thighs. Tell me, I say (another expression I've never used till now), this friend, did you know him well? Uh—No! says the man . . . not well. . . . He wipes his eyes. I thought not, I say, but only to have the last word.

I gaze out the window, hoping the drunk officer will follow, something will catch his eye. Then, miraculous, something *does* catch his eye, the edge of a pink sari moving down the carriage past our compartment. I know, without seeing, the face of this woman. As my companion gathers some excuse around him and hurries out of the compartment, I smile at my reflection in the window. Beyond, a huge blue sign decorated with white fleur-de-lis, reads BIENVENUE AU QUEBEC.

My mother and I are driving to Montreal, to Expo, to pick up my father and sisters. They've done it, they've retraced the old voyageur route, and we are going to greet them with my mother's date squares and a Canadian flag bought on sale in a hamlet west of here. We drive around in circles for a long time, trying to find the right pier. Finally we think we are there, and sure enough there is a dot of red way out in the now huge river and something glints—a waving paddle?— above the dot in the sun. When my father and sisters climb out of the canoe onto the dock, they look huge. My sisters pose like beach musclemen, draw their fists against their shoulders and tell me to squeeze. I curl my fingers over their swelling biceps and suddenly feel very weak indeed. These goddesses of health have also changed color, from off-white to deep amber brown.

Okay, okay, says my father, as my mother offers everyone date squares, we can't hang around yakking all day. He explains that a police boat caught them coming down the main channel, which is illegal, and on top of it, this is the wrong pier. My mother and I ferry their damp smelly packs into the back of the car, while my father and sisters lift up the canoe. Now I notice another family in pale summer shorts and T-shirts, standing nearby. W'ere 'ave you all coming from, the man shouts, and my father's face flushes redder through his burn. A long way from here, he laughs, you probably wouldn't have heard of it. Pardon me? says the man. He has not caught what my father said. My father switches gears. Très loins d'ici en fait, he says, onze jours en canot. The other man shakes his head, takes his children's hands and pulls them along. Well, says my mother, when we are all in the car, you did it, all of you, I'm so proud. This godforsaken country, says my father—we've come to a barrier reading ACCES INTERDIT—how the hell do you get out of here?

This scene replays itself again and again on my window. My father's hand forces the steering wheel. Below, all around us, the car tires crunch and squeal. The canoe, hastily tied on the roof rack, dives forward, back. We brake and then accelerate. Brake, accelerate. Brake. My father's ejaculation: How the hell do you get out of here?

Another scene. Gelid pine and spruce wait stiffly under chill white armor for spring. My father stomping soundlessly ahead, making that possible, pulling the heavy tree.

I cast a furtive glance at the officer bobbing in half-sleep across from me. Now it is I who feel the sudden horror, plead silently into silence: *How the hell do you get out of here?* At Patna the army man gets out, saying he must catch another train. I watch him step down. He wobbles a bit on one foot, then, like a bolt of lightning hit him, stands straight up and walks off. I, too, am getting off at this station where the Ganges widens, but I have been pretending otherwise, packing my bags up in my head as we arrived. Now that the revolting man is out of sight, I jump up from my seat, grab my things and hurry to the door. From here I will catch a bus north to the Nepal border, then more buses through that trainless, nearly roadless land to Kathmandu.

The first car in Nepal was a Rolls Royce, carried part by part by porters over the mountains from India. There were no roads into Nepal then, just one short track the despotic Rana prime minister had built for himself between his palace and government house in the center of Kathmandu. Once the Rolls was assembled, the prime minister himself climbed in and drove away. The people were still watching as the great chariot without horses reared back into sight, tearing a hole in the veil of its own dust.

This is the picture my rickshaw driver speaks, pulling me across the border. He was a small boy then, tangling himself in the quick steady steps of the porters, begging to carry the steering wheel a little, just to touch it. Now he makes three rupees per passenger. He takes a little swig from a tin flask tied to his beltloop, turns to me and grins. Rickshaw gasoline, he says.

Then I am back on a bus, climbing due north up a steep and winding mountain road. I am reminded of vehicular explorations with my father—the throwuppy kind. When we are breaking the back of this mountain, says the man sitting beside me, you will see the beautiful Himalaya and, kneeling at her foot, the legendary city of Kathmandu.

Kathmandu. My stomach contracts suddenly, my hands tear my scalp, my head is between my knees. Is something wrong, meeess? asks my seatmate. I am doctor, can I help? I shake my head violently—no, no!—but that is not what I mean. What I mean is, my throat is filling up with vomit and I can't speak. He *could* help, in fact, by reaching across my back and opening the bus window. He has already thought of that, and as I rise, enormous, like a surfacing whale, and thrust my pouring mouth into the blowing dust, the doctor, stepping neatly across clear social borders, reaches out and touches me, holds his hand, now growing warm with vomit, under my trembling chin. When the hot convulsion is over, a spotless white handkerchief appears before me, a cool hand folds my hand around it and helps me to wipe my face.

Thank you, thank you, I say, I'm so sorry. What keeps me bent out over the open window? Not embarrassment for being sick. But I find I cannot look directly at this man's face. How, I say, turned half-toward him, still gasping an odd mixture of bus grit and fresh air, how do you say thank you in Nepali? There is no word in Nepalese itself, he says. For that you would be having to go to the Sanskrit. This thanking is not so popular in Nepal. Well, thank you anyway, I say. The man bobs his head to the side and blinks his eyes.

At the top of the pass, the bus stops at a little tea shop my acquaintance calls a *pasal*. Most of the passengers stay fastened to their seats or disappear quickly into the tiny dark room within. Come and look, says the doctor and waves his fingers at me as though saying goodbye. He ducks behind me through an overhung path behind the pasal until we emerge on an open knoll. I hang back, reluctant to go further in this lonely place with this man I don't really know. When does the bus go? I worry, glancing back through the tangle of bush. Look, says the man, urging me forward with waving hands. Look. And I do. My eyes open, as if for the first time. What they see is paradise.

How shall I describe this world before me, this lush peak-laced vision, like the lost fringe of some collective dream?

And garlanded about the scene, a red scent of perfect flowers, mercifully slicing the top of my head open, letting me breathe? A scream chirrs off the hills, knocks resounding silence back into me. I remember something. I remember being born.

Dumbly I point into the distance, into the cerulean sea-sky beyond the mountains, unable to say what it is I want. But the doctor seems to know without asking. Shambhala, he says, simply. Shangri-la? I say, thinking I've heard wrong. His eyes smile. I suppose you could call it that, he says. In Buddhist legend such places as you are meaning are called hidden valleys. There are many of them, like your paradise, but not as fine either as Shambhala. In these lesser paradises, it is said, people live a hundred years as a god. But we must think of how they got there in the first place, often by acquiring much merit, by good deeds. After a hundred years or so, their clothes begin to soil and people can smell themselves. It means they have been using up their store of merit. Soon they will die and be reborn in hell, to suffer all agonies they avoided temporarily before. But Shambhala is the last earthly paradise on way to Nirvana. From Shambhala one goes on to perfect bliss. Shambhala lies even beyond where you are pointing, to the north of the Himalaya, maybe in the Kunlun Mountains of Tibet or beyond. Only a very few have found it, says the doctor. The way there is much longer and more difficult; even great yogis and high lamas travel for years, become lost or devoured by demons or are turned back. Only those with greatest wisdom can follow directions and sketchy maps in the ancient mystics' texts. Good deeds, even in compassion, are not enough. To go to Shambhala, a person must even wake up from earthly sleep of illusion, knowing true nature of reality and himself as he really is.

Beside me, the doctor's face is luminous in the late afternoon sun. Then, oddly, the soles of my feet claim my attention. It's as though, through my sandals, my whole foot—the heel, the ball, arch and toes—is pricked lightly by a million blades of grass. As the doctor continues to speak, these tiny blades spark along my ankles, up the front of my calves, behind my knees, along my thighs and hips, my belly and chest, my fingers and palms and upper arms, my neck and chin and cheeks and nose, my forehead. My hair seems to stand on end.

Shambhala itself, the doctor continues, when anyone can find it, is surrounding itself in snow mountains, higher than any bird or lama can fly. Inside that circle lie the eight lotus petal-shaped regions, each having twelve principalities. These small kingdoms themselves are containing many cities with golden pagodas, happy peaceful citizens, all surrounded by green parks and meadows and flowering trees.

Further in still, rising even higher than outer ring, is another crown of mountains made of solid ice. They shine with an inner light. Inside that, in very center of Kingdom of Shambhala, we are finding Kalapa, the capital city. Two lakes in the shapes of crescent moon and half-moon are sparkling to the east and west. These are full of jewels. Scented flowers are floating on lakes; water birds are skimming over. South of capital city, a beautiful sandalwood forest is growing, called Cool Grove. Here is a great mandala made by Manjushri Kirti, first King of Shambhala. It is a mystical circle containing the essence of secret teaching—that mind and universe are one. Oh—but I am forgetting myself, isn't it, says the doctor, we must be hurrying or miss our bus!

Back on the bus, I think of a long-ago postcard from Vienna, addressed to me. The return address: Paradisgasse, Paradise Street. My mother spoke of flowers that cascaded everywhere around them—begonias, peonies, iris, roses—from flower boxes, balconies, stairwells, hedges. It's like heaven here, she wrote, you would love it, except the gardens are all enclosed behind brick walls and wrought iron fences. When I went to touch a rose the other day (I was just leaning down to smell it!), a man rushed out of his house and down his walk, yelling something, waving a trowel at me.

We begin to descend now, brace our hands on the seat in front of us to keep from sliding down. The bus bumps slower, slower, the engine screams. The driver is having trouble, it seems, switching gears. The doctor taps my arm, points up to the roof. Then he points to the window, nods his head sideways, climbs lithely over me and puts his shoulders out through the window. I hear shouting, the doctor's lower body and legs sway limply in the air for an instant, like a hanged man, cut-off view. A flurry, then the doctor shoots straight up and disappears. More shouting, then a head descends, upside down. The doctor? Or a stranger? Pointing in the window at me, extending one hand. Impossible. When the doctor disappeared, the worlds fell sideways, then began to curve. . . . Vertigo? Perhaps—for the first time since I've left home. Motion sickness? Maybe. I can no longer tell them apart. I read once that in a certain period in Russia, epileptics were considered blessed with a mystic connection, a supernatural power—not diseased. What if this dizziness never leaves me? Could I learn to consider my vertiginous state a benediction? Or would this very belief represent a collapse, the darkness under the sunlit cloud my mother warned of. *Don't swallow it whole.*

Fire consumes the body, water extinguishes the soul. How has this knowledge come upon me? I do not stop to wonder now. Now I have a journey to make, a destination to reach. Behind my palanquin lumbers a train of eunuchs, handmaids, royal hairdressers, tailors, astrologers and accountants. Only my husband is missing. Where is he? Without my husband, the raj, father of princes, I am alone. My husband is not dead. How could he die in those barbaric regions, so far away from me? No fire is bright enough to burn his body. Not without me. I have a journey to make, a destination to reach. Shiva blinks. The world in a moment. My husband on fire. Body of my body, alive with flame. Flame licks elbow, knee, shaped calf, fingernail. Licks toe, earlobe, hair. Licks belly, thigh, soft moons. Licks the forgetful rigid. Shall I blink? Shall I close my eyes? In a moment the hot spark of creation. When I jump in . . . When I fly in . . . nnnnnaaaaahhhhhh, but how bright the faces! Cold nor hot. EC . . . (Am I.) STA . . . Thick nor thin. SY! Skin, fine paper searing from my limbs. Inside nor out. (Am I.) Breathless nor breathed. ANHHHH! ANHH-HHAAA . . . A truth I discover: the body eats fire, the soul goes hungry. There is no prayer in fire but water. EEEEIIII-IAAAA! No llaaa in the tongue but rain coming. Rain coming, rain rain RAIN RAIN RAIN—

I jerk awake. I've been asleep or daydreaming. The upside down man is waving frantically now, his face turning red. Okay, okay, I nod and climb up on the shaking seat. The man extends both hands to me, someone must be holding onto his feet. I turn around and sit on the window frame, my feet still resting inside on the seat, and stretch my arms up. Then, like a barnyard cow in a cartoon tornado, I'm zinged into orbit. For an instant I'm suspended, floating slowly down the mountain beside the bus, then I'm yanked skyward in a collective new grip.

The doctor's kind face greets me, he points out famous mountains on the horizon, and surprisingly I know a few. I am not certain how I came on this knowledge; perhaps back home, History left some book or map lying about. It is easier to see and concentrate on what the doctor says up here. The air is clear, it's the view from a magic carpet; below us the grinding gears and pillow of dust seem laughable, somehow perverse. Other men in nondescript shawls and trousers (I can't distinguish who was my savior, now that we are right side up), a family, some young boys, share the roof. A goat sways gently beside me, head high despite her neck rope being caught under her foot. It is not long now, says the doctor, we are coming to Kathmandu. You have husband? The doctor is looking off in the distance. Pardon me? I say. He turns. You have lunch, then? He pulls a little bag from the breast pocket of his jacket and holds it out to me. When I look in, there is nothing recognizable as food, but I put my hand out to be polite. He pours pellets of some kind in my palm. Thank you, I say, and his head wags. I take one pellet, place it between my teeth and bite down. Flavor blazes along my tongue, my nose fills with fire. Beside me, slightly in front, the doctor crunches noisily on a handful of these seeds.

Over there—the doctor points to a dark grove of trees—is where it is customarily to feed our bloodthirsty goddess Kali. I pretend to look where he is pointing, into the deep treed gorge below us, but I am trying to not see. You are fortunate, says my guide, you will be coming to Nepal for Dasain. That is biggest festival of our year, like your Christmas—very auspicious, most joyous time of year. We call Dasain also Durga Puja, for then we worship Divine Mother of our universe called Durga, also Taleju Bhavani or Kumari, the king's deity; destructress Kali; Bhairabi; Gujeswari and many more—all different, but all Durga herself who killed the buffalo demon Mahisa, so that good may always triumph over evil. In Dasain all mother goddess temples are drowning in blood for many days, from thousands of animals sacrificed. We also bathe in holy rivers at this time, make many pujas, offerings. Families visit, give gifts and blessings, we make pro—what do you call them?—parades! Of course all year long the goddess demands blood, and we give little by little. But in Dasain, the blood of joyous celebration is bubbling on the streets!

I do not reply or even allow myself to look at the excitable doctor but try to keep the back of my throat from crawling up. I watch the pedestrians who have begun to collect in the road around us, who turn to look and are swept up in our dust. The doctor nods into the distance. At first I think he means the sparkling river—I nod and smile. You see it? he says, insistent. Yes, beautiful, I say. The doctor looks puzzled. The fire is beautiful? he says. And I look harder. Beside the river, in the dying daylight, a spark. I make out black specks around it. Mourners, says the doctor, sending their dear one through the blazing fire into another world, or if not so lucky, back to this one. He winks, then grows solemn again. I hope for that family's sake, it was not their husband and father. The breadwinner, I say. Yes, says the doctor. And if it is? The doctor flicks his palms up in a gesture of joyless resignation, Ke garne? And the wife? Ho, ho—it is suttee you're meaning, no? says the doctor. That is an outdated custom now. Wives are not jumping on their husband's pyres these days. But it makes me think of that story of an old-time widowed rani, or queen, in English, whose only desire left was to join her soul with that of her husband in his fiery journey. She threw herself, screaming in triumph, to perish on his funeral pyre. Just then the sky was opening up—it seems Indra was feeling playful. Whatever the cause the earth was pounding with rain as even the old men and women had never seen. That fire was put out instantly! There stood unlucky rani, black and soaked, tearing at her hair because she will now have to continue with life. Once the fire was out, you see, so was the rani's duty. It is said she wept day and night until, over many years, tears collected all around her in a deep pool, and she won her wish instead by drowning! But I see you are bored, the doctor says. It is true, these rituals are for the ignorant, who do not yet have enlightenment, as we say, of science, isn't it? No, no, I protest through my still seething mouth, my crawling throat. Not bored. The doctor looks me in the eye to make sure. May I tell you then, he says, about the ultimate, the supreme rite? It is from the Bharat (India, to you), from ancient esteemed Vedas. . . .

His hand makes a little motion near his head. Before us Kathmandu is coming into clear view. The light over the mountains is lifting, one gold cloud reclines—goddess on a bed of nails—over the pagodas' spiked roofs. The sun, which has shone out of reach above us, could be touched with the left hand, if that were polite.

. . . It is very first verses of the *Brhadaranyaka Upanishad,* the doctor Continues. Sacrifice of kings to renew royal power. Here queen takes an important part, for it is in queen such power is staying. That queen is representing refreshment, youth, life, herbs, waters, expansion, creation, food and sacrifice itself. The doctor's long fingers seem to curve the air around them; I search for a memory I can't quite grasp. Now the doctor begins to chant: *Om.* Head of sacrificial horse is verily dawn, eye of sacrificial horse is sun, vital force air, open mouth the fire named *Vaisvanara,* trunk the year, back is heaven, belly sky, the hoof earth, flanks four directions, ribs intermediate directions, limbs the seasons, joints the months and fortnights, the feet days and nights, bones the stars. . . .

The doctor looks sideways at me and winks. I am translating, he says. And now I laugh, fully, heartily, my insides softening down like a new furrow. But the doctor is suddenly serious again. Day, verily, is golden cup in front called *Mahiman,* which arose in respect of horse. Its source is eastern sea. Night, verily, is silver cup behind called Mahiman, which arose in respect of horse. Its source is western sea. Verily these two cups called Mahiman appeared on either side of horse. As a steed it carried gods; as a stallion, celestial minstrels; as a courser, demons; and as a horse, men. Sea is its stable, sea, its source.

The doctor opens his eyes, which had closed as he chanted. In that horse sacrifice, he continues, queen anoints horse, takes its sex organ into her lap and plays at copulation. May the vigorous layer of seed lay seed, she says. Her body, you see, is center of prosperity, children and royal power. This way she brings new life, wealth, good reign to king. But even great kings perform this rite, says the doctor, still does not prevent soul's transmigration. For this reason, the *Upanishad* begins with this meditation to create dispassionate spirit. Meditation prepares for great text itself, in which one may be coming to know Brahman.

I nod my head sagely, glance around at the other denizens of the bus roof. Surely they will wonder at such talk. Copulation with horses! I wonder if the doctor is working up to something. But our rooftop companions stare out over the countryside, or, prone, bend their arms under their heads in sleep.

Coming to know Brahman . . . Now I remember and recite to myself softly, *Heaven, the rain god, this world, woman—*

Man! finishes the doctor. How are you coming to know that?

Children materialize around me, shout Mi-tai! Smile; one small girl takes my hand. Where are you going, memsahib? they ask. Kathmandu, I say. Memsahib, where are you going? they ask again for the sheer pleasure of words. A few more steps (more children gather)—Didi, what is the time? I look at my watch, which has stopped, and say five-fifteen. They scream, giggle to each other, till another one dares: O didi, what is the time five-fifteen? Children run around in front of me, behind, tangle in my feet, almost tripping me, fall accidentally-on-purpose against my heels. Three boys on one bicycle glide in beside us; they and the other children talk quickly among themselves. I am shaking now, under my red pack, laughter mixed with tears. The children grow quiet for a moment, then rekindle their chatter. In a mile or so, I am calmer and begin to chatter, too. What is your name? I ask each one, who then shies away and says something too soft to hear. Then the others pipe up: Ramchandra! they yell. Lakshman! Krishna! Surya! But do not ask me mine. One boy conjures up a tiny live owl and asks if I want to buy. For good luck, he explains. No, you keep, I say, and he looks surprised.

I notice now I am walking more slowly, the children have seen to that; outside our noisy circle the landscape is quiet, green as a cow's dream. Long ago a bus roared into its own smoke. Now sound is damp: a cowbell, a cock crowing on a human shout, the ring in my ears. My father once told me his ears stopped ringing when I was born. Could this be true? And if so, if this were not something dreamed up in my memory over long inattentive years, why have I never asked, When did they start?

On the outskirts of the city, I drop my pack on a stone bench under a pipal tree. Two jangling women under huge baskets of wood come and rest their loads beside me, laugh and laugh at my short calf-length skirt. A third woman appears from behind them, carrying a baby in a shawl on her back. The children do not rest but tag each other around the tree. One boy on the bicycle jumps free, and two more squirm on. The bicycle-for-four wavers across the grass, down into a ditch, where, laughing hysterically, its riders all fall off. A local boy chases a rolling metal cylinder along the road with a long stick, tapping either side to keep it upright.

I think about my hurry to get off the bus; did I offend the doctor? I still think of him as the doctor, although during his rambles he explained, I am doctor of civilized life and growth, engineer to be exact. His true love, though, was the ancient sacred texts of the Hindu.

Feeling the bus slow, I alerted a young man, pointed to

my small red pack under his knee. And in that instant saw it was all I would need. Another man started to haul up my suitcase and large grip. No, no, I said, you can have it, divide it among you. I picked my way around hands and feet to the rear ladder and climbed down the back of the bus to the village street. I had been trying not to look at the doctor, but as I went over the edge his face shone unbearably in the moon. I remember the graceful resignation of his fingers, the shaped gentility in his single word. Please, he said and beckoned me with that strange clipped wave of the hand. *Please.* It was not a plea for himself the doctor was making, I see that now. Nor was it the guardian's appeal to a wayward child. No, it was as if the doctor were again translating, as though all terror and magnificence, the most exquisite torture and horrific pleasure were now designated in this one particular sound.

I shoulder my pack and start down the final mile, secure in the children's ring. I hear laughter behind us and turn; the two laden women have joined our group, lagging a little. The third woman, with the baby, has disappeared. My muscles ache from the long cramped journey; my head swims in a night sea. It occurs to me I could be walking in my sleep.

THE GOD WITHIN YOU

(The Story of an Incomplete Tale)

The Tale

I am your tale. Who but you will tell me? Wrap your tongue around me, Raja. Lick me into shape.

Yet, held in your teeth, breathless, I am ever your tongue's hostage. As such, I pray for release, for breath. Say this, I pray, say that. Again and again my prayer dies on the wind.

While I, I am alive—but only half! Fit now just for prayer, which is foreign to my nature. Perhaps in endless bondage, I have become my prayer. Perhaps breathed, I would discover but the loss of my other half, my completeness. Once, Raja, you began me. Having begun, having told the half that is I, complete me.

The Raja

Friends. My story tonight is not of the past but of the future. It is a story of another world whose events do not fall backward into memory, like the building stones of history, but unfold, one by one, like petals of a flower, and only in dream. Listen then, my people, to the strange history that unfurls slowly, surer than memory, and with the full weight of prediction.

In the remote mysterious Himalayan land of Nepal, where foothills are big as mountains and mountains disappear into the sky, where villages are tossed like grains of salt across the hills, one village shines like a jewel in the heart of the country—a wide lush valley scooped out of the rough hills by the hand of God. This village, greater than the other villages, so great it is like a hundred villages together, is more properly called a city. Its name is Kathmandu. In the middle of Kathmandu is an ancient and beautiful palace. But the palace, for a hundred years, has been without a king. A hundred years ago, his dynasty was overthrown by the present rulers, despotic men all of a family whose terrible power is snapped like a lock over the land. This family, called Rana, usurped the King a century before, promising an end to feudal subjection. Now that same clan has itself become cliquish and tyrannical, isolating the people in their feudal past, disallowing art, music and education, driving them deeper and deeper into a black hole of debt, restricting all contact with the world around. War is the exception, for the poor people by now having great physical strength, no wealth, and being trained to mental obedience, make excellent mercenary soldiers, and the glory and spoils they bring home from their successful campaigns are quickly snatched by the greedy overlords.

Now to the south of Nepal lies the huge and mighty land of India, with whom little Nepal is outwardly friendly, inwardly resentful, and both outwardly and inwardly very much obliged. These two neighbors get on together like the nearsighted elephant and its companion, the pragmatic mouse.

Now, at the mouse palace, three Ranas munch on lavish sweets and good wine and talk among themselves. There is talk of independence in India, says one, stroking his leopard chair rug. This will not bode well for us nor for our investments. We've known of this for some time, says the second. It's best to continue as we have already begun, hedging our bets, massaging those factions in India sympathetic to our government. It will be a bitter blow, says the third, if that socialist Nehru takes over as they say he will. I suppose our own socialist lackeys will think their time has also come.

At the same time, across the land, men, Gurkha soldiers, fan up the hills like ants returning home from war. In the villages, people gather to listen to their tales. But underneath the many stories of bravery and cowardice and horror is one story, unspoken, and for that reason heard more clearly. This story is of a blind man whose eyes are opened, a deaf man whose ears begin to ring with beautiful sounds. The story is of a mute who begins talking, a man without taste or smell who walks by a boy holding a line on the riverbank and smells fish. The story is of a stupid man who suddenly becomes bright as the sun. How do these miracles happen? you may wonder, just as those farmers and petty merchants gathered in the villages wondered. And I say to you in words what the soldiers say to friends and neighbors, not in word but between words, in voice and eye and hand: How different everything is in those foreign lands, different and yet the same! The people must fill their bellies as we do. They pray for luck, prosperity and rain. They hope for many sons. They fall sick and die. They marry and make love. They laugh and shout and cry and sing. They drink water and make water. They suffer, grow old and are released into the sky. But this very sameness gives cause to weep. For in that world, that same but different world, some same men cloud the other same men's sun. When a man goes hungry, it is not always because he does not pull hard enough at his soil. When a man is spit on, it is not always because he's done wrong. And if a man is fat and greasy with good food and great wealth, it does not always mean he has worked his land well.

This is the story, the underneath story the people hear. When the stories end and they turn back to their hovels under an absent moon, they think about the sagas of bravery and courage, of suffering and pain and sacrifice. They remember, despite thinking, the underneath stories told by the feet and eyes and hands. And toward morning, when the dawn is breaking and they haul themselves out of beds that have grown cold, when they sling the water bucket over their shoulders, whose empty bottom they will see again before sundown, they cannot help but think about these people in foreign lands, about the land under their feet they till but don't own and about their dreams. Then over days and months, even idle thought becomes restless, disobedient. Dissatisfaction climbs, like the returning soldiers, up through the southern plains to the hills, up the hills to the very stars. . . .

THE TALE

Telling your dream, Raja, telling me, you fall asleep! You lean back snoring! This crowns my rage. What should I think? How escape, when I'm unrealized, unformed, without choice, owning nothing but myself—incomplete? Yet am I still a goddess, the Goddess of Tales. A plan is coming to me in pieces, a plan to lift silence. To speak yet not to speak. Not to the Raja himself. Not in *his* sleep.

THE BODYGUARD

Tonight, in my dream, a voice. I am the Incomplete Tale, it says. Each night your master, the Raja, begins me, then tires and falls asleep, leaving me incomplete. You know of this? Well, I'm sick of it. Listen. You are the Raja's bodyguard, no? I am speechless. Well then, she continues, please warn him: Either do not begin me at all or, once begun, then finish. And tell the Raja this for me: If he does not complete me very soon, I will kill him.

The Tale

Sneak here and there
Find go-betweens
Travel only at night
Appear in others' dreams
Speak when the Raja sleeps—
The rules of partial existence.

The Raja

Loyal subjects. You will remember how three despotic Ranas with their cousins, nephews and sons, sought to keep their people in the dark shadow of fear and ignorance, exacting obedience and tithes out of all proper proportion. How rulers and ruled were as a mouse living under the shadow and protection of its clumsy elephant house. Now the elephant, between whose feet the careful mouse subsists, is starting to rattle her chains. Yes, the elephant herself has been in bondage these many years. And when the elephant begins to struggle to her feet, when the strong chain links begin to weaken and strain, the mouse, no matter how comfortable or threatened, must herself, perforce, be snapped awake. For the mouse's own life is bound for change.

So into my dream, into this mouse-sized land, a kind of restlessness creeps. The peaceful green hills and valleys become obscured by the smoke fires of meetings. Even at the palace in Kathmandu, a new uneasiness stirs the Rana oppressors from their century-long sleep.

Now the government of the elephant India to the south has had one blurred eye on its great tiger rival to the north for some time. This tiger land, called China, has got a sharp eye on the mouse. The mouse, Nepal, is the elephant's best friend and eyes. Without the mouse to warn her of the tiger's approach and minus her chains to rattle and frighten China off, the elephant can look forward only to her demise. So the elephant, sensing her small friend's lethargy, must wake up the mouse to guard her life.

The head Rana, called Prime Minister, peeks through eyelids swollen shut by high fat cheeks. This swollen Rana, for whom drinking four tumblers of fine dark wine and smoking eight imported cigars, for whom eating three gourmet meals and bedding two beautiful women all in one day are tediously mundane . . . this Rana, feeling the wind of change stirred up by his dreadful companion to the south, peeks out through the small slits that are left him for eyes and sees a little light.

He calls his scribe to him and from his imported rosewood divan dictates the text of a new writ to be proclaimed throughout the land, whose provisions contain moderate reforms toward the elephant India's point of view. This he signs and seals, no longer requiring, as did his Rana ancestors, the seal of the deposed King. He sends the writ with his most trustworthy minister to Delhi, India's seat of government, that foreign familiar land.

That evening, as he disports with the loveliest of his ninety-six concubines, she informs him of three things he had not known. One, there has been another, though minor, outbreak of popular unrest in the hills to the west. Two, the tiger nation China, to the north, has sprung, swallowing up Nepal's closest neighbor and distant relative, Tibet. Three, one of her women friends, maharani of a fractious Rana camp, has overheard her husband speaking with another Rana of the same irritable bent. It seems her reforming lover is about to be overthrown. . . .

THE BODYGUARD

Bad luck, oh, bad luck not to finish! A story must always be complete. Still I was too afraid. They all looked to me, mistaking bulk for courage. As my master's eyes dipped, theirs doubled. One message read: Do not dare! the other, Wake him! But I did not dare, and tonight she comes to me again in sleep. Her appearance has little to describe: a shape I cannot catch hold of, eyes that fade in and out.

Listen, she says, I've had enough. You know as I do the hazards of partial performance. Look you, if the Raja does not finish me tomorrow, I will kill him. And if you tell him what I've said, I will turn you into stone.

My mouth opens wide. I plead with her—be patient. I tell you this: her thick vivid lips demand description.

THE TALE

This interruption of a bodyguard. This frustration of brute stupidity between me and my torturer. *RAAAAAAA!* Trapped in the riddle of my own existence, empty threats, that one neat truth a simple guard cannot seize: How could I, forever incomplete, forever born of his master's tongue, how could I kill him? To kill my teller would kill me. Still I count on simplicity. I'll fool the brute out of body's certainty, wait for him to beg indulgence. I've made up my—my mind. Wait. Yes.

No.

Can't

Wait anymore

Just now

Let me die must

Scream!

THE BODYGUARD

AI, AI, AI . . . her soft lips, quick torn petals. A man trembles in her screaming:

I will become a deadly needle in the Raja's dinner! I will let him go to hell because he has ill-treated me long enough!

If you tell him this, you will become a stone. And if this plan misfires, I have another. I will appear as a spring of clear water when he is tired and thirsty after hunting, and when he goes to drink, I will become an avalanche and bury him alive. And if you tell him this, you, too, will lose your life. If that plan fails, I will appear as a shady tree when he is hot and tired. When he lies down underneath me, I'll crush him to death. If you tell him this, you will become a stone. And if this, too, fails, I will come in the form of a snake and poison him with my venom. If you tell him, you also will mingle back with the earth forever!

Ah, but how my master's unexecuted story ensnares me! If I do not tell my dream and live, I kill my good lord, the Raja. If I tell the Raja the story of the Incomplete Tale, that Tale will kill me.

The Raja

My people. The old Prime Minister is gone. The name of that plotting Rana, barely breathed before, is now blown up full size and shouted out loud. He and his new ministers rule with an iron hand. Everyone, from the boot-licking ministers to the rajas to the poor peasants, is terrified of him. Landholders—Rana relatives and favorites—visit their tillers frequently, stripping away what little revenue and less joy is left in the land. Through the hills and valleys, more and more rumblings of discontent. Also screams, when local Rana overlords on their great horses gallop straight through the flimsy meeting huts, stabbing and beating all in sight.

One day in a village at the edge of the kingdom, a poor farmer, bent double under a heavy load of wood, is walking along. He hears some pounding, hammering nearby, and lifts his eyes from the ground. Some of the Ranas' men are erecting a sign. He hurries back to his village and asks a village elder, a wise man, to come with him to read the sign. When they get back to the spot on the road, the Ranas' men are gone. NA-MA-STE, sounds out the old man, who has nearly forgotten how, WELCOME TO NEPAL. Soon, all over the country, ordinary people are noticing such signs. Those few who can still read suddenly find themselves in great demand.

Is it a trick this Rana is playing, this Rana, who, like all Ranas, has no wish to let them hear of anything outside? Is there some monster or god or demon at their border that the palace is trying to appease? Namaste—I salute the God within you. A most polite greeting. Quietly, because they are not allowed to gather, peasants across the land begin debate among themselves.

Some in the south say they recall a shadow, a darkness that appeared once over the land—the green hills quivered at its touch. As the shadow passed from hill to hill, valley to valley, people at first offered rice, thanking it for the early coming of monsoon. But when the shadow passed over without so much as a drop of rain for their thirsty fields, they looked more closely and saw the cloud was actually the shape of an enormous bird. Another tells of a young woman she once knew who disappeared with her baby from the field where she had been planting. A man says he once found a village elder, a wise man in his district, propped against a tree, headless. But these things are not caused by devils outside our borders, a man protests. Take a look at the devils within! In the meeting hall, a cheer goes up. When the noise dies down, an old man at the back speaks up. What about the giant bird-shadow? Is that coming from our own land? Does anyone here have such a bird nesting in their fields? (Throat clearing, restrained laughter, murmurs.) I say this welcome is a danger. Will this thing interpret friendly greetings as an invitation to help itself to our poor resources? Will it, whatever it is, stay on with us forever, gobbling up our best rice and tarkari, lie around making a nuisance of itself, like too-long-staying relatives? (Laughter.) Endlessly these questions are debated by the citizens young and old, trader and farmer together. Fathers and sons stop speaking over the matter; mothers-in-law step up the war against their sons' wives. But it is grudgingly agreed by all but the most stubborn that a polite welcome is the best course of action. With things as bad as they are, at least it can do little harm.

After the meeting, which women are not allowed to attend, a very shy young woman greets her husband at the door. In bed that night, she asks him about the meeting, what was said. After he tells her, she strokes his arm. This shy young woman, who has never spoken a word about public life before, says, But why are our closed-up masters now opening the doors? Neither her husband nor anyone else can answer.

Back in the palace the Prime Minister himself hardly knows. Or knows too well. The wheel of time has turned beneath his brothers, uncles and him. Despite their delicate investments in India, the Ranas of Nepal must ride this inexorable fact. This demon Rana, before whom even his own mother's heart will skip a beat, grips the treaty paper India has sent. His First Secretary stands beside him holding out a pen. The Prime Minister stabs his name at the paper and flings his chair back. That bastard Nehru will drive us to the ground, he says. . . .

The Bodyguard

My master's story twice unfinished since the dream. Twice have I rescued the Raja. The first time, when his voice began to fade, I offered food to keep him awake. But he refused and fell asleep. Next day at suppertime, as the Raja was about to eat, I stopped him. There in his food I found the needle. That night, telling his tale, my master motioned for a pillow. I brought the pillow and some water, praying to every god I knew. But the Raja ignored the water and fell back in the pillow, dozing. Next day, after hunting, we came on a beautiful cold spring. Go on a little further, I said, and I will bring you even better water that comes in my magic bottle. I stooped and drank, then filled up the bottle. Sure enough, as the Raja was drinking at a safe distance, the spring became an avalanche crashing down.

The Raja

Now, ever since the elephant can remember, the tiger has lurked around, tempting the mouse's uneasy loyalty with promises of better security, more food, a more comfortable house. While the mouse, finding her unique position useful to bribe the elephant to drop tidbits, has remained mostly aloof. Over the years, however, the mouse has grown dopey and lazy, allowing the tiger quite close, forgetting her debt of gratitude to the elephant for the fine sheltering body that provides her house.

So now, when India feels Nepal scurry beneath her, signing the limited treaty on one hand, rising in arms on the other, India knows she must leave nothing to chance. She must keep pressing Nepal, get an assurance of her loyalty and new promises of reform. To do this she must not seem to side with either the government forces in her tiny neighbor or the forces of unrest. This is the origin, then, of Prime Minister Nehru's unbending middle way proposal sent posthaste to Nepal.

(Back in Kathmandu, a dark figure, the King, steps like a ghost from his Rolls Royce, walks up two steps and disappears. The huge carved doors of India's embassy slam shut behind him. The signal has gone out.)

That night, in a small town in the south, a hundred or more shadow-men crawl on their bellies across the dark. Some have long glinting sticks in their hands; others have curved knives—or nothing.

Suddenly bright lights blaze out like suns from the district Rana palace, framing their bodies in cruel dawn. There is fire everywhere, coming out of the long sticks and from the guard posts around the grounds. The men on their bellies squirm backward, arched up, like snakes leaving old skins. A few stay there on the field, motionless in their skins....

The Tale

Speak for who cannot, Raja. Who is beyond words. Hear her silence.

The Bodyguard

Oh, if only it were my place to speak! What I would say to my master before the assembly is this: All of us, your loyal listeners, are dying to hear this story end. Great Master, why not finish? Night after night, your marvelous tale, told with such skill and beauty, departs unconsummate, unsatisfied, born of great hope, growing faint, left to die incomplete.

But neither truth nor prophecy is mine to speak. Body is where I belong, not speech.

The Raja

One fine day, while the Ranas enjoy a feast of fried chicken, French cheeses and a lewd play in the great hall, a messenger arrives from Delhi with Nehru's proposal for compromise. The messenger hands the envelope to the palace guard, who turns it over to the palace doorman, who takes it in to the chamber guard, who passes it to a low-ranking Rana seated near the door. Eventually the important looking missive arrives at the Prime Minister, who begins to choke, as fate would have it, on a bit of chicken bone. When he recovers he calls for his golden letter opener, and before the entire hall he reads:

The Government of India sends greetings to its good friend and neighbor, the Government of Nepal. As always we wish you prosperity and desire that you be independent, progressive and strong. To this end we urgently propose the following measures as acceptable to you and certain unofficial but important organizations in Nepal. . . .

The Bodyguard

Day after day I must watch the Raja closely, while pretending nothing unusual is going on. This I can do. But what can anyone do against prophecy? Those fine final words whispered at dead of night in my brute's head? I am not stupid. To stay awake, to ignore the goddess, would mean sleepiness during the day. If I were to sleep then, my master would surely die. Take today. My master found a shady spot under a tree. Boy, he called to me. Spread my carpet down. Wait here while I rest awhile. Just then I heard the crack, pulled my master away as a huge branch fell to the ground where the carpet lay.

The Tale

Twist of bone under muffled skin. Soft crush of nerve. Tumbled in your tongue, Raja, body without speech.

The Raja

That bastard Nehru will drive us to the ground! The very words of a new man in my dream. Himself of peasant stock, this fellow has risen among the restless to lead the struggle. This leader of the people speaks before a nervous crowd:

While Nehru sits, no, *impales* himself on his *middle way* fence, friends, we will prove our strength, our power, our determination in the march toward freedom from the Rana grip. One minute Nehru champions our cause, the next he says we are too sympathetic to the communist tiger and disallows our transport of arms. I say, to hell with his flattery, his *support,* given by the tongue and taken away again with the hand. My friends, we don't need him! King Tribhuvan, deposed and rightful heir to the throne, is on our side. With his blessing and God's, we shall strangle our Rana oppressors, if we must, with our own hands!

Thus begins the long fire that snakes across the lush hills and valleys of that mouse land, Nepal. A steady roar, like thunder, with discrete claps riding on top. Everywhere fire sticks blaze. The ones in dirt-colored uniforms, the Rana armed forces, are far superior in numbers, weapons and fire stuff. But the others, in tattered dhotis or thin fitted shirts and trousers, some even in old Gurkha uniforms, have more heart. They push hard across the country from the south toward the capital, Kathmandu.

This night, sleeping in a sympathetic village where they've temporarily retreated, their leader dreams of King and country. He dreams the King is not an emergency guest of India but a prisoner. The sovereign cannot send the rebels so much as a hopeful letter, for his hand is invisibly stayed.

Then the dream rolls backward, and he witnesses that spectacular event heard about but not seen. The King had been whisked out to Tribhuvan Airport, then swallowed, with his colorful entourage, by India Air. He dreams the silver Air Force Dakota lifting, lifting on the sky, its metal sides curving into green scaled wings, its nose becoming the nose of the King, its forward windows his eyes.

When he awakes and steps out of the generous house, he knows the trapped King will give in to Delhi's proposed compromise. After this night of dreaming, everything and nothing will be changed. The rebels will rise sporadically, then cease. The Ranas will concede their partial demise. The King will assume control, renaming the old theocracy a *partyless democratic state.*

Nameless leader of a nameless army who has fought so long to keep the many forces from staging undisciplined assault in his heart, he picks up his gun from where he'd left it politely outside the door and wanders silently down the village street, collecting a band of silent men. Have they, too, dreamed of the King? Have they, too, chased a dream through the night then misplaced it? Will they, too, recognize on future's face the failure of their predictions? As he wanders on into the morning, His troops wind an undulant line behind him, bearing incomplete revolution heavily on their backs. Speechless, each feels the morning like a heavy stone. It is not morning to them, but the lingering twilight of tropical sundown. They are finished, except for their passage at arms. The incongruity of their situation is not lost on their head. He breathes heavily then gives a short sigh or laugh. Royal revolution, indeed. Revolution without end.

The men begin to slip off and hide in the hill jungles, according to plan. Tonight they will regroup and force again....

The Bodyguard

If. If. If. How duty becomes bondage. I must save the Raja, and mutely. If. If. If. My tongue stilled in a web of condition. One danger remains: the deadly snake. If I could only warn the Raja or wake him. Instead I must take the Raja's safety, and mine, in my own hands. Tonight I sneak into the Raja's bedchamber, hide in a dark corner. Soon enough my master enters. Soon enough he falls asleep beside his queen.

I watch. Watch and wait, the future incomplete.

The Tale

I am I am I am I am. Coil of pain. Limbs not my own twist beyond belief. My breath sunk from the realm of possible, open-mouthed, I pray for extinction.

The Bodyguard

Here she comes, slithering snake. Fangs showing. Misery coiling up the Raja's sheets. *KATAK!*

The Tale

I am I am I am I am. Tale without head. Blood sprayed on the Raja's sleeping queen. Wake up, Raja, wake up! Feel something writhing in your sheets? With all respect, it is your tale, not finished with you yet. Lean down, bodyguard, wipe the queen's cheek.

The Bodyguard

Snake blood on the sleeping queen! I must wipe it off before my master sees. Oh, all the demons of hell! For just as I am leaning over the queen, my master, the Raja, wakes up.

The Tale

Wake up, Raja, and rage. Feel my writhing. Look to your bodyguard. Look to your queen. See how he lays his hand upon her cheek.

The Bodyguard

What could I say? For if I told the true story of the Incomplete Tale, I would become stone.

The Tale

Like a stone, your bodyguard refuses to speak. He turns red only and stammers. Silence to you, Raja, means one thing. So you order him hanged until dead.

The Bodyguard

AI, AI, AI! Death waiting within me, close, so close to the skin. The rope breaking my neck if I do not tell the Raja. If I do, I'm petrified. *AI, AI!* Before my execution, the Raja grants me one wish. This I take, saying, I want audience with the Raja. To die with a clear conscience, I will tell everything—of the Tale, the dreams, deceptions, the snake, how I rescued His Excellency time and again. And now the hour for my audience has come. I am taken in chains before the Raja. *Well?* he says, frowning. And I say, feeling the hard pebble grow inside me, It all began with a dream. . . .

The Tale

Guard, tell the sad story of the Incomplete Tale
Become stone, the waiting within you
Now, Raja, my story-seeking torturer
Now will you repent?
Will your tale end?

Printed on paper
containing over 50%
recycled paper including
10% post-consumer fibre.

Printed in Canada